JUXTAPOSITION PARADOX

CHARLES R. STERN

Grey Wolfe Publishing, LLC
PO Box 1088
Birmingham, Michigan 48009
www.GreyWolfePublishing.com

© 2015 Charles R. Stern
Published by Grey Wolfe Publishing, LLC
www.GreyWolfePublishing.com
All Rights Reserved

ISBN: 978-1628281248

Library of Congress Control Number: 2015955113

Juxtaposition Paradox

Charles R. Stern

Dedication

To Sam for all of the support, encouragement and love she has so generously given me in the writing of this book.

Acknowledgements

My deepest gratitude for the help and support I have received from my daughter Lia Stern and the assistance I have received from Professor Janet Langlois and Diana Kathryn Plopa.

CHAPTER ONE
Gimme Shelter

The Community Mental Health office was a rather stark cave where, over the years, the winds of misfortune had left their mark in the dust from internal battles between conflicting personal demons. This, despite the fact that the place had been constructed within the past ten years for its current purpose. John Doe had spied the date on the cornerstone in front of the building adjacent to the entrance when he emerged from the bus.

He sauntered into the waiting room for the first time and stopped motionless for the strike of what seemed to him like at least two minutes on the clock of surprise. Wonderment stalled him long enough for his irises to adjust to the dimness of the lobby. He was struck by the tableau spread out before him in the din.

What a contrast, a transition from the brightness of the blue day to the dusty, dingy yellowish green light of the lobby. He urged himself forward just a few steps into the stillness. It was morning out in the sun, but inside it was a dusky artificial twilight.

He felt compelled to blink his eyes, dilating each to its maximum, and stepped slowly again to what was obviously the receptionist's desk. There was a sign-in clipboard on the ledge in front of the sliding glass window that kept the receptionist separated from the lobby. He wrote his name and checked the box that indicated he was a new supplicant at this institution. There was a second clipboard with forms to be filled out with personal information. He took it and scanned the foreboding cavern for an empty chair. The patrons were escapees from a Fellini film. Hollow blank eyes stared at someone or something in the indeterminate distance. A few squinted right through the magazines on their laps.

This is no place for anyone with night blindness or anyone for that matter. They'd need a leader dog or a cane.

His vision adjusted as his eyes circulated the room. There were three lonely unoccupied seats looking just as depressed as half of the poor folks slumped in the others. The empty seats were surrounded by a population of patients who had positioned themselves with one vacant seat between them. The seats projected a rule that no one should sit next to anyone else unless there was no other choice. Even then, the odd man out had to endure the humiliation of being in the uncomfortable position of a rule breaker. He had no choice but to sit where there was a patient on his left and one on his right. He was surrounded by the weight and numbness of overly medicated psychosis and depression.

He felt as if he had entered a different world. One where the populous was marooned in their own separate islands of misery. Beyond the dimness, the room seemed institutional. There he was in the waiting room with recently outdated and thoroughly worried magazines on small tables. Apparently, the shallow pockets of the State budget didn't allow for the purchase of reading material for patients. It was obvious to John Doe that the workers, out of compassion for the patients, had brought their own personal magazines in from home after they had devoured them. In fact, they looked as though someone had swallowed them whole before regurgitating them back onto the side tables at the ends of the rows of semi-matched chairs. He knew this because all of them had the addresses cut out of the corners on the front covers and some of them were only one or two months old. There were, of course, the obligatory government published brochures scattered about. John Doe speculated that about one percent of the patients actually read them and they did so out of boredom.

John Doe looked around at the ghastly reproductions of pastoral scenes on the walls. They were mass produced and made to appear as though painted on canvas. They could have been purchased at any mall kiosk or online for very little cost. They were probably purchased in bulk to adorn all government offices. *They like to conceal their cheapness by the term "cost effectiveness".* He thought they were gauche. Most of them were painted either by hand in a third world country assembly line for a dollar or two per twelve hour day or they were printed off in mass production on a specialized printer that mimicked real paintings. The walls were all painted a neutral beige, but the florescent lighting cast a yellowish tint. There were two windows in the room, but their shades were drawn because the windows faced the East and the morning sun was too hot and squintingly intense for the solemnity of the place.

Maybe they want to keep the patients swaddled in what they probably tell themselves is "subdued lighting." They probably fool themselves into the belief that it's soothing rather than dysthymic and sleep inducing. A metaphor maybe, for keeping the patients calm and ...well, subdued. He wondered about how the patients felt. They were already made sluggish by their depression or their medications. *Maybe they don't notice or care.* It's ironic that a community mental health clinic has to block out the light. *Isn't this a place for enlightenment?* He realized that there was a difference between reality and the metaphor, but he wondered if it sent an unconscious message, just the same.

The individuals in the waiting room were mostly silent and either staring off into an abyss of blackness to match the mood or they were staring with empty glazed eyes at the outdated magazines while trying to look interested. Some just stared. It was likely that most magazine articles of any length had been left only partly read or if read, they were soon forgotten in the hazy side effects of medicated brains. Several individuals appeared disheveled. One woman had the magazine in her hands upside down. Another woman supplied the entertainment. She had obviously not been taking her meds. She was too busy quietly arguing with her hallucinations to notice her surroundings. So much so that when her name was called she didn't hear it. The receptionist had to call her six times before she shook herself free of her reverie.

John Doe waited for two hours before the receptionist called his name.

The receptionist was a middle-aged woman, five-feet-ten or eleven inches tall, with an obvious wig on her head that was long and straight. It reminded John Doe of an Asian look, but she was not Asian. *She is shaped rather, like a pyramid.* Her head seemed dwarfed not only by the wig but by her enormous body that seemed to widen as it rolled toward the floor. In fact, her face seemed to be disappearing, embedded in undulating masses of overgrown flesh. She wore a kind of Mumu dress that was green and white with large red flowers on it. It tented over her body and the design made her seem even more mountainous. She seemed to be in pain just sitting there. John Doe felt sorry for her and wondered how much longer she could continue to work at this job.

As he approached her desk, she followed him with her eyes, but her head remained still. She arose from her much-too-small perch with herculean effort. There was much groaning and cracking of knees while she steadied herself with the help of the desk. She had to stand for the count of exactly one thousand eight before she could take her first step. Apparently part of her job assignment was to lead the new patients to the intake office. She said, "Follow me, please." There was no modulation in her voice. It was labored and nearly breathless.

Jesus, I hope she doesn't have a heart attack right here in the hallway in front of me!

She waddled to the door, unlocked it, and ushered John Doe down the hallway. She tipped back and forth with each step, barely bending her knees when she walked. She was trying to steady herself on the deck of a ship that was pitching and rolling. She huffed and puffed and groaned and creaked. He could hear her indistinguishable mumbling in the draft of her wake.

Poor woman, what a struggle! I guess everyone has their own private hell. She certainly is not enjoying anything about this. He looked away so she wouldn't feel stared at even though she was navigating ahead of him. *She might be able to see behind her.*

John Doe noticed the inspirational posters displayed on the walls. The ones that leap out at you depicting scenes that were supposed to match the inspirational quote or statement at the bottom. You know the kind. They read, "Courage" and there's a picture of an athlete in a downhill slalom skiing competition spraying snow in a rooster tail behind them. The kind of poster that makes you say, "That sounds right. I should be like that!" and three steps later it sinks beneath the waves of conscious memory.

Inspiration is worthless without an accompanying goal for motivation to drive one forward when the going gets difficult and the feeling of inspiration dies away.

The receptionist led John Doe shuffling through the hallway maze to the office of the intake social worker. She was puffing and gasping for breath.

Poor planning, the intake office should be right inside the lobby door. Maybe they make her walk new patients down the hallway to get her to retire or maybe have a heart attack. Either way, they would be rid of her and couldn't be accused of discrimination. John Doe wondered if it would be weight, gender, or age discrimination. Regardless, it seemed inhumane and mindless, especially for a supposed human service organization.

They eventually arrived at the port of call where a sign on the door read "Mental Health Intake." As they entered, she silently gestured to the chair. John Doe thought that she put so much emphasis and authority behind it that he could almost hear the command you'd give to your dog to "SIT!" *I reckon she's too mean to retire or go on disability.* He was reminded of the bumper sticker that read "The meaner you are, the longer God lets you live." *Maybe even God fears her.*

John Doe did her bidding. He sank deep into the now spring-less, and almost cushion-less chair well-worn by thousands of derriere. He found himself sitting right up against the social worker's desk since the office was too tiny to have room for a chair to be pulled back to a comfortable distance. His legs had nowhere to go but under the desk that seemed more like a table. He felt nervous as it was. Being bossed around by the receptionist was not helping. *I wonder if this is a good idea after all. The place seems unhealthy.*

He surveyed the room and noticed the name holder on the desk that read, Julie Harper, M.S.W. John Doe surmised that it stood for her graduate degree, Master of Social Work. The light in the office was dim or subdued. John Doe sat quietly for a moment contemplating what to say. The social worker sitting across from him began her intake evaluation and psychosocial history.

"I'm a little nervous," he said, "this is my first time in this office or any other counseling facility for that matter..." he paused. "At least as far as I can remember," he followed up.

The social worker, Julie Harper, was a thirtyish redheaded woman with horn-rimmed glasses that were too large for her face. *Weren't they fashionable in the 1920's and again in the Beatnik and Buddy Holly 50's and maybe the early sixties? Maybe they are back in style... maybe. Maybe her prescription was the same as her grandmother's from whom she had inherited them.* It struck him at first that they gave her the appearance of an owl when you considered her long straight nose. His thoughts went into neutral for exactly one second. *But no, actually, she looks more like a bug. A red beetle.*

She was thin and maybe five feet tall... maybe. She wore almost no makeup. John Doe thought she may have had on a little lip gloss. He wasn't sure. If so, it was so understated that it was barely noticeable. *It's probably chapped lip salve.* Her ears boasted heart-shaped gold post earrings. There was a tiny gold chain around her neck that sported a matching heart shaped charm with a fake diamond that appeared to weigh it down at a forty-five-degree angle. She wore a simple white blouse. When he had first entered the office, he could see beneath the desk that she was wearing black slacks and sensible flat shoes.

There was one picture on the wall. It was one of those forgettable inspirational posters. John Doe couldn't remember what it said after he left her office. There was a corkboard on the wall in back of the desk that had various notes of different sizes and from different pads of paper tacked up in a disorganized manner as though they were targets in a pub during a drunken dart throwing contest. She clearly had little time or inclination to put them in order and simply tossed them up there in a fit of procrastination. There were a couple of photos tacked there too, depicting her and fellow staff members looking empty-eyed bored with forced smiles at a probable office Christmas party.

Her elbows rested on the well-worn desk. It had files piled high on both sides of her such that she appeared to be peering at him through a tunnel. There was a computer tower on the floor that looked to be about six cyber generations too old with the monitor sitting on a side table that apparently used to be an ancient typewriter stand. It had numerous post-it notes plastered around the edges of the monitor that looked like passwords for various programs. Its keyboard was lying on top of the old, very large monitor.

There was an old landline phone with several extensions indicated by the number of visible buttons. It was so well worn that the numbers on the keypad were faded, and in some cases, obliterated from seemingly centuries of use. It was perched precariously, leaning on the computer monitor at about a thirty-degree angle, since there didn't seem to be any room for it anywhere else. John Doe reckoned that she was supposed to have had the stacks of paper files typed or scanned into the very old and slow computer. The computer looked old enough to be ready for the technological boneyard. Of course, legal documents had to be printed out and kept as hard copies, too. This was the backup plan ever since the mainframe hard drives had failed and files were lost. *Maybe these are just unfiled legal documents. Maybe she calls them, "pre-filed" cases,* but to be fair, he didn't see a file cabinet, nor was there room for one.

Ms. Harper's head and just the tops of her shoulders were all that were visible peering over the desk. Her chair was obviously broken and she couldn't get it to stay cranked up high enough for her to sit comfortably. John Doe guessed that she had requisitioned a new one or at least a working one months or maybe years ago, but she may still have a long time to wait. She was so diminutive that it seemed as though she was very far away.

This can't be the light at the end of the tunnel! He amused himself. He had just told her he hadn't been in a similar situation as far as he could remember. "As far as you can remember?" she said with a mild surprise in her voice. He didn't respond right away like most people Ms. Harper had dealt with. *Does he have something to hide?* She frowned slightly. *Or is he too paranoid and reticent to reveal anything about himself?* "Well, we can start with your name."

His head was bowed and his shoulders slumped. He finally said, "I don't know."

"You don't know your name?" Her eyebrows lifted.

She leaned a little farther into the tunnel making her shoulders disappear below the desk. Her head seemed to be floating there, suspended in the middle of the desk. *An eerie sight.* John Doe was reminded of an old horror film or a bizarre Science Fiction movie. He expected her head to swivel around three hundred and sixty degrees; spew pea soup, and her voice to suddenly sound like Mercedes McCambridge with laryngitis.

He had been ushered into her office by the receptionist so Julie Harper hadn't yet looked at the referral sheet the receptionist had handed her that now lay on the desk. His name was the third one down the list since he was her third appointment.

She glanced at it and then at her roster of patients for the day that also lay on her desk. "Oh, I see that they have listed you as a John Doe, and your appointment was made by the shelter. Why didn't you tell them your name?"

"'I can't remember anything before several months ago," he said.

"You have amnesia? Even for your name?" She said it with such disinterest that there was barely a question mark punctuating her words. It was as if she'd heard that one before. Well, actually she had.

"Yes. And I'm not completely sure what happened," he replied.

He leaned forward as though he was going to whisper a secret into her cave. She reflexively leaned forward too. Now they were both leaning over the desk. Two heads in a floating world. Julie Harper glanced down and was suddenly startled to realize the decreasing gap between them and quickly sat back in her chair. John Doe stood his ground. He didn't want to seem intimidating, but he didn't want to look like he was retreating from his position either. He wanted to seem non-threatening, but sincere and forthright.

For her part, Ms. Harper seemed to be vaguely unaware that she was attracted to this unusual man but regained her professional distance. *He is attractive and interesting.* Then she shook herself mentally, *you've got to watch out for that type.* But then she had heard this sort of thing before. *Don't be fooled by his charm,* she told herself. She peered at him from the distance of her own tunnel of professional skepticism. She had seen such cases. They were always men, most of whom were hiding out from the law or they were too paranoid to reveal anything about themselves, but they eventually revealed their real names. *Usually.*

"All I know," said John Doe, "is that my first memory was when I was laying in the street bleeding from a lump on my head late at night. The fog and dizziness seeped into my brain, overwhelming my consciousness. I assumed that I was hit on the head by someone because there was some blood. I remember that my head hurt and I reached up and felt a wet lump. I looked at my hand." There was a long pause while he mimed touching his head in stunned, slow motion and then lowering his hand and holding it out while surveying the blood. His mime was so realistic that Julie Harper could see red on his hand. She shook her head and the blood was gone.

He expected the social worker to ask a question, but she remained silent. She was trying to make him uncomfortable enough to tell her the truth. Besides, she didn't want to telegraph anything he could use as fodder with which to embellish his story.

John Doe said, "I was lost in the mist of fear and confusion."

"Maybe you were in a traffic accident," she finally said.

John Doe sat quietly for a moment in deep thought. "I don't think so. My head was the only injury. If I had been hit by a car, wouldn't there have been other signs of it? You know, other injuries or wrecked car parts in the street. And where was the wrecked car?"

Her head, heavy with her characteristic skepticism, dropped slightly as if to say, 'Oh boy, here we go with the stories.' "Well, maybe you were in your car and hit your head in an accident. You could have hit your head on the steering wheel. Someone could have stolen the car if it was drivable."

John Doe's brow wrinkled into a frown of disbelief. "Maybe," he started to say in a slow questioning voice, "but wouldn't the airbag have prevented that? I was bleeding from a lump on the back of my head. There wasn't much blood, but I was obviously hit from behind. If the car was hit hard enough to knock me out, an airbag would have deployed. It's likely that the car wouldn't be drivable unless the bag was cut out. But there were no cars around and no airbag remnants laying in the street." After a brief pause, he said, "there were no emergency vehicles either."

"I see." Ms. Harper leaned forward into the tunnel's shadow again with a quizzical expression. She was trying to appear intensely interested now. Her bug-like appearance seemed more pronounced than ever.

John Doe couldn't get that insect image out of his mind and it was difficult for him to hold back the flood of laughter that welled up in his mind at the caricature-like image. She looked down while she tapped her pen on the desk in an arrhythmic cacophony that echoed in his mind.

There was a thoughtful silence, except for the tap-tap-tap of her pen, that he thought was much too strident and it went on much too long. It seemed to him that she was trying to beat his story into submission, or at least into a shape she could cope with. Each tap fired off high pitched blasts in his throbbing head. "Did you have any I.D. on you?" she finally asked.

He answered without hesitation. Maybe a little too quickly. "No. I didn't have a wallet or any way to identify myself. Believe me, I've thought about this for months." A long awkward pause engulfed them again.

"I see, but why did you wait for many months to seek help? Why didn't you go to the authorities right away?" she asked with an indistinguishable edge of triumph. She sat back in her satisfied chair and rested her tiny chin on tented fingers. She was looking down through her glasses that had since slid to the tip of her nose. Gazing at him between the stacks on her desk she looked to John Doe like a giant gargoyle atop a very small church steeple.

"Well..." He hesitated for a thoughtful moment trying to brush aside the gargoyle image. "I woke up alone with a lump on my head and bleeding in the street with no I.D. There were no cars nearby. I was dazed and blurry. I didn't know where I was or even my own name." He hitched his shoulders up and opened his arms wide palms pointing toward heaven in a half pleading and a half "I don't know" gesture.

"I didn't know whether someone wanted me dead for some reason. Maybe they left me there believing I was dead. I just didn't know. I was frightened and confused. I was afraid someone would come back looking for me. I just wanted to get out of there in case whoever did it returned. I had no idea what had happened. I didn't recognize anything. The whole place seemed unfamiliar to me. So I ran and hid until I could travel here. I figured it would be easier to get lost in the mass of people here in such a large city. Maybe I'd be more anonymous and it would be less difficult to stay hidden if someone was after me."

"Where were you when you awoke in the first place?"

"That's just it. As I said, it was unfamiliar to me." *keep up damn it!* "I ran and walked for miles, hiding out in wooded lots and behind buildings and houses. I don't remember where I started out.

I was dizzy and confused. I passed out a couple of times and woke up in a field once, and another time in an alley. I was terrified and desperate. I didn't know where I was or who I was. All I could think of was that I had to flee. Paranoia drove me to escape a stalking phantom."

Julie Harper put on her skeptical face again and peered out from behind those enormous glasses that, John Doe thought, extended two inches beyond her face on either side like those fake ones you can get at a novelty shop.

"How did you get here with no money and no I.D?" she inquired with a dollop of cynicism.

"I got a ride from a trucker and I eventually panhandled a few dollars and cashed in some abandoned bottles until I had enough to catch a bus here."

"How did you survive without money after you got here? Did you find a job?" Now she was an even more skeptical gargoyle atop her steeple.

He looked into her eyes trying to summon sincerity. He answered without hesitation. "No, I was too scared to get a regular job. If someone was after me, they might find me. I was pretty paranoid."

Tap, tap, tap again, but this time she was tapping her pen on the right temple of her bug-eyed goggles. This simply drew further attention to how they distorted her face.

"I washed dishes in kitchens in the back of small greasy spoon restaurants a couple of times, but I never worked at the same place for more than a couple days and never at ones that asked for I.D. or insisted on reporting the income to the government. I was paid under the table daily."

"How did you do it?" She slid her glasses back up her nose with the middle finger of her right hand unconsciously flipping him the bird. The symbolism did not escape John Doe's notice.

"How did you manage?" she frowned, causing her specks to drop to the end of her snoot again.

She moved her pen to intersect her lips by ninety degrees as if she was trying to prevent them from telegraphing too much of the skepticism that she had inadvertently already revealed.

John Doe was a little more animated now. He was gesturing with his hands and facial expressions. His voice had a wider range and modulation too. "I was okay hiding out and panhandling for a while. I slept under freeway overpasses and in parks. But the weather turned cold. I had to install myself in shelters and warming centers at night. I also stayed in public libraries and other buildings, churches when I could, and twenty-four-hour stores. I went to soup kitchens for food whenever possible. There were many times when I went to the outdoor farmer's market and picked up some discarded food and cooked it over a fire I'd set in a trash can in an alley or a remote field away from where cops were likely to find me. I found a group of homeless folks at one point and stayed with them for a short time."

"What were you wearing? Maybe that will give us a hint about what you did for a living or what your socioeconomic status was."

"I had these shoes and socks on. They weren't worn out like this of course. At the time, I had some off-the-rack chino type pants and a cheap buttoned-down collar shirt. Of course, they were dirty and torn in spots. That was it. No wallet, watch, phone or anything else."

"Well it sounds like you weren't poor, but you probably weren't rich either. My guess is that you were in a low-level white collar job. That is, if you were employed." She hesitated before her mouth extruded her suspicions. "It is possible that you were a low ranking criminal." She paused for a reaction, but none slipped out. "Your vocabulary is good, though; so I think you were probably educated beyond high school and you most likely have a college degree or at least some post-high school education. Maybe some kind of technical training. You appear to be middle-aged so you probably haven't been in school for quite some time unless you were required to attend continuing education for your job. What made you come here to seek help after hiding out for so many months?" Her voice maintained the distance of her reserved professional monotone.

"The people who run the shelter where I'm staying talked to me about seeing someone from the community mental health agency when they found out that I had amnesia." He sat forward and looked her in the eye with a pained expression that pled for sympathy. He wondered, though, whether she could even see his expression in the dimly lit shadow between the steep graying cliffs of folders that framed their faces.

Her voice softened a little and she sat slightly farther forward in her chair again. "How did they find out you had amnesia?"

"I had given a false name until I slipped up and returned to the same shelter with a different name than the one I gave them on previous visits. They confronted me and my confession eventually slipped past my lips and there it lay on the table. I admitted that I didn't remember my name or where I came from. That's how I ended up seeing you. I guess that's why they said I was a John Doe. By that time, I had made up quite a few names for shelters and temporary jobs. I couldn't remember them all. I had to come up with them on the spur of the moment because I was afraid to be identified, I didn't use the same name when I moved to a new place. But I had to use the same name at each shelter when I returned there. I didn't want to draw suspicious attention to myself. I guess that's why I slipped up that time. There are only so many shelters and I accidently gave a different name at that shelter on a subsequent visit."

"You could have rejected the advice of the shelter workers. What made you decide to come here after you had been avoiding detection for so many months?" A hint of skepticism returned to her voice.

"I wanted help, but I didn't know what to do. They told me at the shelter that you had to keep things confidential and that I wasn't going to be turned over to the police or exposed to danger if I talked to you."

"Well, that is true, with the exception of when we think a person is mentally ill and in danger of hurting themselves or others even unintentionally." She half-heartedly offered reassurance.

"I don't want to hurt myself or anyone. I just want someone to help me remember who I am and why this has happened. I need to fill in the gaps." He looked down and tried to convey the feeling of sadness for his loss of identity. "I didn't know I could talk to anyone who is kind and understanding like you in confidence. You seem nice and I think I can trust you." John Doe wanted to flatter Julie Harper, social worker, so she would be as much help as possible.

A Cheshire cat smile appeared on her face and there was a gradual brightening of her eyes. She tried to maintain her professional distance, but couldn't help feeling the impact of his praise. Besides, he was a good looking man complementing her on her personal demeanor and professional skill.

The social worker typed his name as John Doe into the electronic record on her computer with the keyboard on her lap. She called him John from then on. She also typed "homeless" with the shelter's name in parentheses under the address section. She had to put "unknown" in the blanks that asked for age and date of birth and in most of the other sections. Under "cognition", she wrote, "above average intelligence." Under "appearance" she put "well groomed" and "attractive." He was "alert and oriented." There was no sign of a major mental illness. Memory deficits were his only problem. She proffered a preliminary diagnosis of "acute amnesic episode", assigned him to a therapist, and made him an appointment with a psychiatrist for a routine evaluation and a doctor to clear him medically. She handed him the business cards of the various professionals with the appointment times scribbled on the backs along with a bus card.

Clouds of unknowing obscuring the original mind.

CHAPTER TWO
Karl Otto

It was an extremely challenging and difficult day. Work had ganged up on him with a vengeance. It felt good to leave the stuffy office and walk out into the cool air. He was suddenly aware of the sweaty swamp in his pits and the dampness that had formed on the back of his neck as it cooled quickly in the penetrating breeze. He loosened his tie and pulled his collar open to the length of two inches. His body began to breathe again and he felt resuscitated.

Karl Otto had finally extricated himself from that world. His car steered itself down the ramp of the parking structure to the exit and, set on auto-pilot, it headed for home. An electrical storm was brewing. It hadn't started raining yet, but the storm was closing in because the thunder claps that followed each blast kept getting closer together. He counted to one thousand and two between flash and roar.

A bolt hit about ten feet from his car and interfered with the electrical system. He had to switch off the auto-pilot. He took charge of the manual mode and drove the familiar route that he had difficulty remembering toward home. He had relied on the auto pilot so much that he had difficulty retrieving the route from the dark recesses of his brain. *One more thing my brain has to deal with.*

"Three miles or so to go... I think," he said aloud.

He found himself taking deep breaths that were more like deep sighs and discovered his shoulders were stretched extremely taught over his muscles. He realized he was hunched forward over the steering wheel and forced his back to straighten. He was tired. Exhaustion was chasing him home after a difficult workday, and a recent lack of sleep. Now he had to readjust to the world he was about to enter. A task he was not looking forward to. His brow was furrowed and tight. *Out of the pan, into the fire.*

Karl Otto worked at a financial investment firm in middle management. *"Middle management is the correct term for this position."* He flashed back to his childhood. He was a kid playing the game of keep away they used to call "Monkey in the Middle." The other kids stood in a circle throwing a ball or beanbag back and forth high over his head, the kid in the middle, the monkey, was supposed to intercept it. Basically an almost impossible task. Now that he thought about it, he remembered being the monkey just about every time because he hung out with those kids who were a year or two older than he was. "You're elected," they'd say. As if it was some kind of honor. *The honor to be humiliated.*

At work, he was in charge of several employees who did a lot of grunt work on the phone and on the computers. He felt the heft of their perpetual complaints about the crushing weight of too much work for the time allotted. He was the dartboard of blame for the impossible deadlines and sudden shifts in the direction of their projects that left a debris trail of unfinished work in the frustrated cyber dust. He was blamed, despite the fact that those orders came from above him. His superiors were relentless with so-called "new" ideas for the company that were the same old ones wrapped up in bright new packages with sparkling labels. The ones that previous bosses had tried but failed.

This must be the way the Christians felt being sacrificed in the coliseum. Nowhere to run and nowhere to hide. The crowd is in a frenzy. There's no way out of the chaos disguised as some kind of order. Fight or die! Karl Otto felt a little nauseous thinking about it. He puked up a little lump of fear into his throat, choked, and swallowed it back.

His superiors were always scrapping one plan or idea for what they perceived as "better", but this caused his department to have to scramble and change everything on a regular basis. His employees were always complaining about the workload and the stupid policies. He truly was the middle management monkey with too much work and everyone riding his ass. It seemed lately that he hadn't had any time off. He often had to work nights and most weekends to his wife's chagrin and outright indignation. He knew she was lonely, *but what can I do? It isn't practical to quit or find a new job at this stage of my career.* "Now that I think about it," he heard himself say aloud to no one, "I'm in the middle between work and Grace, too." There was a pause, but no one responded with the exception of three rain drops on the windshield that he didn't notice.

Grace was his wife who constantly complained that he had to work late and often on the weekends. They had several raging arguments late at night. She seemed to always choose times to talk when he was so exhausted that he couldn't think straight. Sometimes he even fell asleep mid-sentence, at two o'clock in the morning. Of course, Grace took this as his disinterest in her feelings and their relationship. She would awaken him with tears and loud screams of frustration spewing epithets hissing through her perfectly straight clenched teeth while she expressed rage and disappointment. She even struck him on the chest once. It didn't hurt physically, but he got the message and it was emotionally painful. He felt discouraged.

To be fair, Grace falls asleep during sex sometimes, but somehow that doesn't seem to count. Of course, I dare not mention it in my defense. I have to stifle myself like Edith Bunker.

However, they did have some more rational and intimate talks about that situation recently, when he was awake and still lucid and had his wits about him. He felt these discussions went better than he had anticipated. She appeared to be a little more understanding, but he didn't really think Grace had a true change of heart.

Karl Otto feared that there was a divorce in his future. He felt as though his wife was on the verge of leaving him due to boredom and frustration. She no longer had the children to occupy her time and she was bored with her work. She worked to help with the expenses and the tuition for their two college students, but she hated her job.

Grace was upset when she confided in him, "The empty nest is getting to me. I want, no, I need, more stimulation and novelty in my life. I feel abandoned. I know on some level that my anger is unfair, but I have sacrificed enough, and now it is time to start something new for me."

He sympathized with her and he feared she'd find someone else who would have more free time and could pay more attention to her. Then she'd leave him. Maybe she already had hooked up. After all, he worked nights and weekends. She could be out and about and he wouldn't know it. He shook his head to rid himself of the image and shuddered. He pushed a button to maximize his speed and struggled to leave these thoughts behind. But they seemed to be chasing him all the way home.

During the last fully awake and lucid conversation he had with Grace he explained that he couldn't risk losing his job. "There aren't any positions out there that would pay me a comparable salary. Even if I could find another job with commensurate pay, it would demand just as much of me or possibly even more than my current job. Besides, I can't support your lifestyle and spending as it is. There's also the college payments for Joy for the rest of this year and Jimmy for at least at least one more year." A tiny bit of understanding seemed to creep in.

Maybe she just shut up while she is quietly planning her escape. She promised to think about it, but she might simply pack up and leave me.

She sometimes said she was out with girlfriends, but he wondered if she had taken a lover. There were a few times when she stayed out so late that he arrived home ahead of her. Still, he tried to be cautiously hopeful after their recent discussions. *I do love Grace very much and I don't want to lose her.* That was the bottom line for him. He would do anything for her within reason. *Well, at least not too far beyond the bounds of rationality.* But he couldn't quit his job. That would make things worse in the long run.

Karl Otto pulled into the driveway. He pressed the automatic garage door opener and had the sensation that one experiences when one is about to enter an alien world. The garage light failed to ignite, but the lightning flashes lit the inner sanctum for a moment. He pulled in and pressed the button on the remote again. The garage door closed leaving the outer world behind.... For now.

The lightning and thunder, I calculate, are signaling that the storm is upon us.

He turned off the engine and sat there in the dark garage for a few minutes breathing deeply trying to drain work out of his brain and ward off panic before entering the den of his beautiful but ferocious lioness. He needed a moment before having to be the gladiator facing Grace and the sharp teeth of her problems. He closed his eyes and squinted them tight, and let them go trying to relax, to decompress. Her world was always fraught with surprises, most of which were overwhelming, at least Grace thought so.

I have always been attracted to Grace, partly for her ability to express her emotions as well as her intelligence. That has always made her more interesting. He had definitely wanted her company and her still very attractive body. But that was before she had turned all of that against him. A second middle management job.

His memory flashed back to his childhood when he often felt as though he was an observer. Or maybe a participant observer in his own life. He would observe other people's behaviors as well as his own. He always watched every move his body made and every thought his brain could concoct. Somehow, he never felt he belonged anywhere completely. The world he moved in felt, at least in part, alien to him. He remembered looking in the mirror in the bathroom and wondering if the Karl on the other side felt the same way. He seemed to move the exact same way Karl did.

Except, he's left handed. I wonder what that world is like.

While Karl Otto sat there, he faded through the veil of somnolence into the world of sleep. As he did so, he thought he heard some music. Maybe he was listening to his own dreams or maybe it was the sound of the car's engine running on after the ignition was turned off, even though modern cars don't run on after the ignition is shut down. Maybe it was the radio or the stream from inside the house. He made a mental note to check it as he drifted off.

Thunder startled him awake.

He reckoned he was only in the realm of the god of sleep and dreams for a few minutes before Thor's angry thunder unceremoniously returned him to this one. He felt a little odd but chalked it up to fatigue. This garage world seemed like a portal between the stress he just left behind and the one he was about to face.

Now he was about to enter another world that seemed to have become an alien landscape.

He slowly opened the car door and stepped out. He girded his loins tightening the straps on his mental gladiator's armor and prepared to enter the arena. But he was a tired gladiator and he wasn't certain that he was up to the battle.

Karl Otto was a reasonably good-looking middle-aged man about six feet two inches tall weighing in at just under two hundred pounds. His hair was brown with some red highlights, but much of it had begun to turn gray or fall out. There was a male pattern bald spot developing on the top rear of his head. His dark navy blue suit was rumpled with some coffee stains and in serious need of a trip to the dry cleaner, a plan for which he never seemed to have the time to execute. His shirt was light blue and his tie was a paisley pattern of various shades of blue and white with some dark red and gray. He wore black plain-toed shoes and socks that matched. As he walked, he projected an air of dignity and self-possession that he did not feel. He felt the weight of time and stress pushing him earthward, making each step seem impossibly heavy. Whenever he found himself so burdened that the gravity of his world caused his posture to sag a little, he'd straighten himself, take a deep breath, and slowly exhale. He tried to return to an upright and locked posture and to at least appear to level off and relax.

I sometimes wonder if my appearance of self-assuredness gives Grace the permission to pummel me in the belief that I'm so strong that I can't be hurt.

The only light in the garage was the one streaming through the window in the door that connected the garage to the house and the occasional flash of lightning that leaked through the little windows in the automatic garage door. Karl Otto slid through the door into the house feeling as if he were entering enemy territory in his own home. *It seems odd, to feel so much intense love for the woman who increasingly acts as though I'm the enemy.*

There was a stairway leading down to the basement to the right. A left turn at the top of the stairs would lead to the kitchen, and straight ahead with a jog to the right, was the living room. He took off his coat and hung it up on the anticipating hook at the top of the basement stairs next to the door. He stepped into the living room where his wife usually sat waiting for him watching the stream. She wasn't there and the stream was turned off.

"Grace? I'm home."

"I'm in here." A voice came from the kitchen. She sounded... *What was it? Surprised? Cautious?*

It was then that he became aware for the first time of an unfamiliar odor. *Is there something cooking?* He noticed that the living room was clean and tidy. His eyebrows shot up in surprise. This was completely unexpected. *That's odd. I'm the one who usually has to clean up around here. Did Grace hire a housekeeper?* He made his way to the kitchen and found Grace barefoot at the stove with an apron on and stirring something in a pot. The cat, Algernon, was circling in and out around her legs making a path that resembled the mathematical sign for infinity, between them.

When Karl Otto entered the kitchen, the cat scampered away ten feet, sat on his haunches, and starred at Karl Otto as though he was a stranger in a strange land. He remembered when they had gotten the beast. Grace wanted to call him Algernon after one of her favorite books. The name apparently means whiskers or mustache or something like that. The odd thing was that the book's title had to do with a stupid mouse that became smart through modern chemistry. Maybe she had hopes for the cat. He didn't mind the name though since it was the first name of one of his favorite authors, Algernon Blackwell.

Another flash of lightning followed more closely by a clap of thunder. He heard Algernon fly down the basement stairs as the rain, blown by the daunting wind, began to fall heavily on the roof and beat on the windows trying desperately to get in.

More oddness, Grace rarely cooks anything. I'm the one who cooks. But when I'm late getting home from work, which is quite often lately, either I have to take us out, we order delivery or I pick something up on the way home. Sometimes we heat up leftovers from the recent take out. Now that I think of it, she didn't call to ask me to bring home a takeout dinner tonight.

"What's happening around here?" he asked with a tone of pleasant surprise substituting for the puzzlement building up deep in his gut. Grace turned toward him with an expression on her face that Karl Otto didn't recognize. *She seems to be excited to see me and a little hesitant or nervous...Maybe shocked?* He noticed that under her makeup, her face was blanched and her eyes dilated. There was a nearly imperceptible quiver in her voice.

"Why whatever do you mean?" She looked at him with, what he thought, were questioning eyes and she seemed to stumble over her words just a little. This was unlike the Grace he knew.

Suddenly her demeanor changed and she began to speak with a slightly forced but lilting, eye flashing, and sexy tone. She hesitated and looked him over head to toe, as if she was evaluating him. Karl Otto thought she had an expression of puzzled disbelief on her face. She tipped her head to her left slightly, she turned off the burner, and slowly removed her apron. He noticed that her hair was let down from the usual bun or pony tail. She sauntered over to him swishing her hips slightly.

Grace threw her arms around his neck, tipped her head back slightly looking him in the face with a bright-eyed, seductive smile. But there was something else. *A hesitation maybe?* It seemed as though she was seeing him for the first time. It was as if she was testing her own senses to prove that he was real. Karl thought her expression had shifted, but to what?

What is it? She seems almost relieved to see me.

She said, "Honey, I feel great and I have been thinking all day about how I have neglected your needs. I've been too wrapped up in my own problems." It was then that he saw some mascara out of place as if tears had been whipped away sometime earlier. "You work so hard for the kids and me and you've always been here for us. I've been thinking about how much I really have loved you and how little of it I've shown."

Her arms hugged him tight and he crushed her in his. *Maybe a little too tight.* It had been so long since he had felt such genuine physical closeness and he realized at that moment how much he had been missing it. He stroked her hair and her cheek and placed his hand behind her neck and slowly and gently pulled her lips to his. He moved both hands gradually down over her body and planted them firmly on her butt. She felt his total presence, solid and complete.

He was puzzled. She hadn't been this loving and seductive toward him in years, maybe ever. *Does she want something? Is this a miraculous shift? Have our recent conversations had an effect? Has she started seeing a therapist? Maybe she has she been kidnapped by space aliens and replaced by one of their drones? She doesn't have a twin. Does she?* Whatever it was, he was encouraged. No, he was excited!

Thunder raged in the background. Lightning flashed. The rain was now a deluge and roared like Niagara Falls, but Karl Otto did not notice. "To what do I owe this honor?" he said with a little too much enthusiasm.

"Can't I simply want to please my man?" she said through what seemed to Karl Otto a genuine smile.

He found her hips pressed against him. Intense arousal gripped him. He wanted her. He always wanted her, but her interest seemed to have waned over the course of their marriage. But now…! It was as if the storm clouds had parted and a little chunk of heaven fell out.

She is still so beautiful.

"Don't you want me?" she said with a coquettish tip of her head and slight flip of her hair.

He couldn't help himself. He couldn't believe the sudden change in her. Her sidelong glance was so stimulating that he thought he'd burst if he couldn't have her. He felt the rush of boiling blood within. His heart was pounding in his throat. He read the signal loud and clear! It had already turned from amber to bright green! His mind said, *take it slow. Don't blow it by going too fast out of the gate. Pace yourself for the long run.* But his body said *go, go, go!* The flag had been waved at the starting line. She had cleared the runway and the track was open ahead. His engines were revving awaiting the final signal to pull his foot from the breaks.

He wrapped his arms around her and lifted her up and carried her to the bedroom. With his back to the bed, he stood Grace on her feet facing him. He surveyed her still very beautiful form for a minute before he proceeded to strip her naked. He didn't move too fast or too slowly. He wanted the moment to be a Goldilocks moment. Perfect. Neither Greyhound fast nor tortoise slow. *I want it to be just right.* He was struggling with his urge to ravish her on the spot, but he knew this would cause him to blow past her needs.

She had started to unbutton her blouse. He reached out and finished the job and followed up the task by unclasping and removing her bra. He lightly tweaked her breasts and cradled them in his hands while he bent down and slowly kissed and briefly sucked each nipple. He defied his urges and took his time. He detected a ripple of pleasure washing through her. She unzipped her skirt and let it drop. It was then that he realized she had no panties on. She stepped out of her skirt and kicked it aside with one bare foot. He started to remove his shirt while she knelt down and unzipped and unbuckled his pants. He stepped out of his loafers. With one smooth motion, she slid his pants and boxers down to his ankles. He stepped out of them and kicked them aside along with his shoes. He was about to take her to bed when she pushed him down on it and removed his socks. He sat there. She was still on her knees. She looked up at him. He looked at her. She didn't say anything. He didn't say anything. They gazed at each other. She firmly grasped his very hard self with both hands and surveyed it. He was out of his mind with desire and pulled her up to him. They slipped under the bedcovers that had been left folded down and shared the most erotic and satisfying sexual experience of their entire relationship.

Karl said, "did you get what you needed babe?"

"Sure did!" she said, "I really needed that. I loved it! I love you."

Something in her voice seemed to signal that she was happy, but maybe not completely satisfied. He wanted her to be supremely satisfied, especially now. He wanted to leave no orgasm unturned. He held her tight with one arm and fondled her breasts and nipples with the other. Another small quake rippled through her.

"I thought so," he said. He pulled her close and pleasured her. She moaned and her hips started to move almost automatically.

"Oh God!" she cried.

He was so surprised and delighted that he felt excited again. He felt like a teenager. He entered her for a second time.

She felt as though she was soaring, flying! This was something she had never felt before. She had never surrendered to her own pleasure and certainly not to him so completely. She had never given herself to anyone so fully before either; never trusted so completely. She had never even felt so strongly the urge to give pleasure. In fact, the more pleasure they gave each other, the more their own pleasure grew.

She was finally exhausted. She said, "I can't go on. I'm spent." They lay holding each other. She looked at him. Her dilated eyes were pools of delight. He looked at her and grinned. "I love you," she said softly. She was beaming back at him.

He felt as if the sun had just come up after a long Kodiak winter. She placed her hand on his chest and nestled into his arm. It felt as if their bodies and minds were melding into each other. He stroked her hair and cheek then he kissed her on top of her head. "I really love you, Babe," he responded.

She started to say, "I've missed you…" She stopped in midsentence.

He said, "You've missed me?"

"Well," she stammered, "I've missed being with you like this."

They lay in bed and talked for an hour before sleep captured them and they eventually let go of each other and rolled over into their respective slumber positions. But they felt swaddled in the residual closeness of their bodies. He rolled to his right and she to her left as sleep deepened.

Exactly an hour later the scales of Morpheus slowly fell from Karl Otto's satisfied but sleepy eyes. He stretched, yawned, and rolled over. His gaze settled on his lovely radiant Grace. The cat was lying on her hip. Algernon stirred and looked at him with feline disinterest as though to say, "Annoying!" He slowly slinked to the edge of the bed, jumped down, and sauntered out the door flicking his tail in disgust as if to say, "After all it is *my* bed!" And, "She's mine you know!" Karl Otto shot a sarcastic smile and flicked his own tail back in mock retaliation. Grace was still asleep.

Beautiful, Angelic... despite the drool and the quiet squeaking snore. But even that seems cute now. He drifted back into dreamland. Satisfaction and exhaustion engulfed him.

Something indefinable woke him again at 12:33 AM. He squinted at the clock and turned over and looked at Grace again, half wondering whether last night's excitement was a dream. She had been so different. It was sudden. Nothing subtle about it. He whispered, "I love you" and kissed her cheek. She stirred and nestled deeper into her pillow in the same way she had buried her face in his arm. The squeaking stopped... for a moment.

Karl got up and went into the bathroom, relieved himself, and washed up and, when he walked into the kitchen, he realized that he was starving. They hadn't eaten any dinner; in fact, he had skipped lunch at work that day to attend to an avalanche of unfinished projects. He couldn't get anything done on them until his boss left for the day. There was no more rushing into his office demanding one thing "stat" and then another "drop everything" for "priority surgery." Karl Otto thought his boss was a frustrated physician. "Probably a neurosurgeon," he told the wall. The wall remained impassive. Maybe it didn't find the joke funny. *Maybe the analogy is wrong, maybe zombie is a better one....* "Brains! I need brains!" He laughed at his own joke. The wall remained poker-faced.

The pot of food Grace had been cooking earlier was obviously inedible by now. If it had ever been. He sniffed it and his head snapped back. "Whew! What *is* that?" He heard himself say aloud. "Maybe we should keep it for insect repellant," he mused with a chuckle. A wrinkle of unintended disgust infused his face. He wasn't sure what it was, but there was a cookbook on the counter out of which he assumed she had tried some new mysterious recipe. "Well, a recipe…. Maybe. Remind me to burn that cookbook!" He heard himself say aloud to a phantom secretary.

"Oh well, it's the thought." He paused for revision. "Strike that," he said under his breath, "it's the effort that matters. It was a loving gesture at the very least. I guess." And, after a longer pause he said, "then again, was this some kind of brew concocted by a witch she met?" He put the pan in the sink and filled it to soak before it hardened into a rock… "Maybe she was making a doorstop!" He chuckled again. Apparently he had to laugh at his own jokes. No one else did.

He looked in the fridge and found leftover chicken that still appeared edible… barely. He nuked it to sanitize it and sat down to eat. He poured himself a beer, too. It seemed like a celebration or something. He went into the living room with the remainder of his beer and turned on the stream with the sound low. He flipped through the channels, but there was nothing interesting on. He finished his beer and turned it off. He thought about writing a love letter to Grace, but stopped. Algernon climbed onto his lap. "How," he wondered in a whisper, "could I possibly express my love, excitement, and gratitude in mere words? It all seems beyond meager literary expression. I'll write something and edit it later. If it's no good, I'll just scrap it." He found a pen and a legal pad in the desk drawer and touched pen to paper. Just then he thought he heard the music of…

What is that? It sounds similar to a harp. It's like that instrument we heard at the museum last year. It was that presentation of ancient musical instruments. What was it called…HMM…I think it was a Lyre.

He stopped and looked around and cocked his head to listen. It didn't seem like an electronic alarm or a watch signal. "Could Grace have a new ringtone?" It sounded like an actual

musical instrument, but ethereal. It stopped. He shook his head.
The Lyre began again, but he decided to ignore it.

CHAPTER THREE
Jeremy Therapy One

John Doe sat in a well-worn stuffed chair made uncomfortable from thousands of psychologically impaired butts. He felt the ghosts of former therapeutic lives permeating the office. His chair faced his therapist's. There were no physical barriers between them only their mental walls keeping them apart. The desk was placed off to the side facing one wall and it was piled with books and papers. There was a small bookshelf with amnestic dust covered reference manuals with their own contingent of forgotten phantoms lurking within. They probably hadn't been touched in years since most of the information in them was outdated and more recent data was available by computer.

Jeremy Lincoln a psychologist with M.A. after his name, which meant that he had a master's degree in psychology, was to be John Doe's therapist. He was a tall, somewhat overweight man in his forties. He wore wire-rimmed glasses that seemed too small for his head. The thick lenses that looked to John Doe like the bottoms of coke bottles made his eyes appear too small and beady for his face. They made his melon look oddly distorted. His receding hair was thinning in the middle and graying at the temples. *His hair looks like it used to be brown*, John Doe thought to himself after he saw a few strands that hadn't yet turned or fallen out. His forehead was large and flat, but his nose was long and straight. He had a razor cut mouth with almost no lips that formed an almost perfect, straight line. It was neither a smile nor a frown. It left the impression of an expressionless poker face that made him difficult to read. *He reminds me of a character straight out of Sesame Street with the exception that he's not yellow, green, or purple.*

The psychologist always wore a white shirt and one of two ties that John Doe noticed were clip-ons. His slacks were always black and somewhat disheveled and so well worn that the seat was shiny. He wore badly scuffed black tennis shoes and matching black socks. John Doe surmised that Jeremy was recently separated or divorced since there was an obvious band of white skin on the ring finger on his left hand.

The psychiatrist had diagnosed him with psychogenic amnesia secondary to psychological trauma.

Jeremy Lincoln began by reviewing John Doe's history, what there was of it. All of what he could remember, anyway. He inquired about the circumstances that brought him there. "So, John, what brought you here today?"

"The bus."

"No. I mean what problem compelled you to seek our help?"

"Doc! I was kidding about the bus." He was sizing up the therapist too. *A little lacking in a sense of humor. And maybe a little naive.* John Doe explained his predicament.

"I awoke staring into the dark abyss of amnesia. I didn't know who I was or how I ended up laying in the street with a bleeding lump on my head. I was terrified. I imagined that someone might have wanted me dead. I was dizzy and I fled through the fog. I was in a daze for two or three days and I passed out a couple of times, but I don't know for how long I was unconscious. I eventually made my way here, where I could fade into the crowd in the larger metropolis. I stayed in shelters after months on the streets and finally came to the clinic." He paused for effect. "That's the nutshell version Doc," he said. "That's about it."

Jeremy said, "Man! That must have been scary! I imagine it was worse since you lost all memory of your identity. It's amazing that you managed to survive for so long before seeking help."

"Well doc, I was hoping my memory would return after a while, but I was discouraged when it kept eluding me. I was afraid to tell the cops what had happened, fearing I might be in trouble. I feared that whoever did this would find out I was still alive and try to finish the job."

"Why did you seek help at this time, then?"

"I was tired of living the way I was on the streets and in shelters. It was getting cold out there. The social worker at one of the shelters told me that you guys would keep what I said in confidence. Every step I took was a stride into an unknown future, leaving a trail of questions behind, fading one step at a time into the foggy past. You know how it is Doc, when you're on a treadmill each step goes nowhere and the previous step disappears about three feet to the rear."

"I see. That's very frustrating." He was silent for precisely one second to let his attempt to increase rapport sink in. "So I assume that your goal is to recover your memory. Correct?"

"Yeah. I want to know who I am and I want to know and understand what happened to me. I'd like to resume my life if possible. That is, if it's worth resuming the way it was... Whatever it was."

"I see," said Jeremy Lincoln, M.A. "I wish there was an easy answer to your dilemma, but there are some techniques and approaches that we can try that have proven somewhat successful in the past."

"Somewhat?" The room suddenly became oppressively thick and dripping with syrupy doubt and trepidation.

"Yes. There are no guarantees. Some people seem to have benefitted, but some have not. It's a difficult phenomenon to study because the cases are so few and far between and most of them have brain damage. So, because yours is not a case of brain lesions, we can try some things that will probably help, but don't get discouraged if there are intermittent steps of success mixed with periods yielding little results."

John Doe felt a shiver flash down his spine. He wanted to hear a forecast with more clear skies of certainty and fewer clouds of doubt. He had hoped progress would be more rapid. He expected some kind of therapeutic magic. "Can't you or someone just hypnotize me to unlock the memories, Doc?"

"That's a sensitive and controversial issue. There is the possibility of the hypnotist creating or stimulating an unintended confabulation."

"Confabulation, Doc?"

"Yes. Sometimes an individual will fill in a gap in their memory with what they think must have happened or someone may lead them to believe it happened. A so called, false memory. So, if hypnosis is used in cases like yours, it has to be done very carefully and it has to be precisely recorded. That's in anticipation that you want it to be accurate and it is especially important if there's a possible legal case involved."

"A legal case Doc?" John Doe suddenly felt an uneasy grip of insects wrestling in his stomach. He felt nauseous and threw up a little in his throat. "This is going to take much longer than I thought!"

"Well John, you don't know why this happened and you suspect foul play. So we would have to be careful. In any case, we wouldn't try hypnosis until all other things have been exhausted and you have remembered as much as possible without it."

"Okay Doc, whatever you think might work." John Doe hid his disappointment in a pocket he had manufactured in his brain that he had long ago unconsciously reserved for such things. He suddenly felt like he was in some kind of floating alien world where the future was vague and blurry.

Jeremy Lincoln was impressed with how John Doe had found creative ways to survive on the streets. *He doesn't seem to be the type to have the wherewithal to manage the street life. He seems like an intelligent man, but he doesn't strike me as street smart. He is too open and his responses aren't what I'd expect from someone who lives out there. People like that are usually more suspicious, even paranoid, at least at first. They certainly don't open up so quickly. Could he be conning me? But why would anyone who is paranoid do it like that? If anything, it seems, he would shy away from coming to therapy and fear opening up so easily.* Doubt spilled out of his mind and his supply was depleted. *No. He has to be legit, but naïve. I have no reason to disbelieve him.*

****

Jeremy Lincoln, the psychologist, was flashing back in short-term memory to the origin of his doubts. He had been in a meeting earlier with two other therapists and the intake social worker, Ms. Julie Harper, MSW. They met periodically with Dr. Donald Suiminski, the supervising psychiatrist in a case conference they liked to call a team meeting.

Dr. Suiminski was the psychiatrist who examined John Doe. He said, "I don't see a need for psychiatric hospitalization and the report from the examining internal medicine physician, doctor Raam, said there were no pressing medical concerns." He told the treatment team, "John Doe does not appear to be a danger to himself or anyone else. No medications have been prescribed since he doesn't appear to be delusional or hallucinating. His judgment was intact and his concentration was within normal limits. The only problem seems to be his retrograde amnesia. His memory has been fine since the blow to his head, but a complete blank before that."

"A CT scan of his brain was completed in order to determine whether John Doe had brain damage from the blow to his head. The report says there was only a tiny residual scar on his head, but the examining physician noted that it had been six months or more since he had been struck and there was only a little blood. That indicated that the bleeding was probably subcutaneous. There has been ample time to heal such a superficial wound and his body had reabsorbed the blood. Therefore, the lump on his head had disappeared long before. There is only a small residual scar on the left occipital area of his skull."

Julie Harper was the first to speak up. "I have a funny feeling about this guy," she said. The room, it seemed to Jeremy Lincoln, suddenly got cold and dim whenever Julie Harper spoke up, especially in front of Dr. Suiminski.

"What is your 'funny feeling' based on?" Dr. Suiminski asked.

"It's just a feeling. I guess it's based on my experience mixed with intuition. His story is too pat."

"We'll see if his story holds up. Whether he's consistent or there are flaws and contradictions," said the good doctor. His gaze turned to John Doe's therapist. "I understand Jeremy, that you have been assigned the case."

"That's correct."

"Well, check it out. Look for gaps and inconsistencies in his story and his demeanor."

"Will do, Doc." There was a brief pause before Jeremy spoke again. "So, the amnesia is due completely to a psychological cause?" he asked. He felt the cold stare of Julie Harper, who always seemed to be trying to one-up everyone in Dr. Siminski's presence and her primary target seemed to be Jeremy Lincoln. He and Ms. Harper had a very brief tryst years ago when he first started working there, but he put a stop to it because of the guilt over being married and because he found Julie Harper an angry and negative woman. Besides, he really did love his wife despite the problems they were having.

****

When Jeremy met with John Doe later, he said, "as far as we can tell there is no physical evidence of a traumatic brain injury. The report on the scan of your brain from the neuroimaging department was negative."

John Doe said, "So there is nothing there?" he smiled.

"No, they didn't find a thing. The CT scan report was negative," the therapist said.

"Nothing at all?" he smiled.

"No. Not a thing."

The therapist missed the joke. "Well, I knew I was losing my mind Doc, but I didn't know my brain was missing!" he joked.

Jeremy laughed half-heartedly wondering if he was joking or if he was delusional. *He did smile when he said it. He must have been joking....Probably. Well, at least he can laugh and make jokes. He can't be profoundly depressed.* The session ended and John Doe left the office after Jeremy obtained the name and phone number of the shelter where he was staying.

Jeremy Lincoln worried and fretted about how to help his patient all night. He tried to place himself in John Doe's shoes. He slipped in and out of fitful sopor all night. *I wonder how it must feel to have no memory of yourself, the life you had before, and what happened to you, especially after a violent attack. Bewildered, scared... no, terrified, and confused.* There must be tremendous internal pressure to regain his memories from the darkness and recover the awareness stolen from him by the identity thief of amnesia. *It must be like standing on the shore of the ocean peering out and wondering what it's like on the unseen opposite side and whether he'll ever reach the other shore. He's stuck with who he is now without benefit of the self he constructed in the distant past. That self is fashioned by the beliefs and impressions of others, the so called "looking glass self," on top of his own reactions and experiences. Every step John takes leaves the fading past in his wake and each step forward has no background reference to gage his trajectory.*

It was a condition Jeremy understood professionally but found personally difficult to grasp. He paused for his revelation to slam into his cerebral hemispheres. *Is that why he can't remember who he is? Is he unconsciously trying to escape from his previous life and who he used to be in that context?* Jeremy Lincoln finally felt himself slowly being sucked down into the quicksand of sleep at three o'clock in the morning.

CHAPTER FOUR
Karl's writing

Karl Otto slowly emerged into a state of alert sensibility and gradually realized that his face was flattened with his left cheek down on the desk. There was some drool. He wiped his mouth with the back of his hand. The clock said 5:59 AM. He didn't remember dozing off. The cat was nowhere to be seen. There was a crick in his neck and he rubbed it hard. His right arm was numb and he had dropped his pen. He surmised that his discomfort was from his unusual sleeping position and shook his arm to regain circulation.

He looked down at the legal pad. There was one word, Grief. "Grief? What the heck! I was writing a love letter!" He tore the sheet off and crumpled it into a tight ball, tighter than necessary and deposited it in the trash can.

He felt a strong pressure to drain last night's beer. He abandoned the desk, got up feeling the rust in his knees. He was the Tin Man after such an uncomfortable snooze. "I need oil!" he said in a whispering mock scream. "But this definitely isn't Oz. The gold from the Yellow Brick Road was cashed in years ago." He smiled at his own joke, but no one else, even the audience in his head, and least of all the cat, found it amusing.

After he amused himself, he hobbled to the half-bath near the front door so he wouldn't disturb Grace. She needed her sleep so she'd be fresh for work later. Karl Otto washed his hands, slouched and stumbled toward the bedroom. He wanted to look at Grace while she slept. Somehow that usually made him feel relaxed and warm towards her. Maybe it was the look of total relaxation on her face when she slept. Maybe it was the look of angelic innocence and vulnerability. Maybe it made him feel protective of her. He wasn't sure, but he wanted to experience it.

Karl peered into the dark room. When his eyes began to adjust, he realized that Grace wasn't in the bed. In fact, there was no sign of her. He flipped the light switch by the door. There was no indentation on her pillow and her side of the bed showed no sign that she had slept there. He checked their bathroom, but she wasn't in her sacred lair.

He said, "Grace?" There was no answer. He yelled, "Grace?!" No answer. He wandered around the house looking for her, but she wasn't in any room and she wasn't down in Algernon's underworld either. "Where could she have gone?" She didn't need to be at work until nine o'clock

Karl went into the bedroom again. The bed was still empty. The clock on the night stand shouted "it's only 6:15 AM!" *Maybe she went to work early. Maybe she remembered something she had to do and had to get there early to complete it. She probably wouldn't have wanted to wake me up.*

He noticed her closet door that seemed to be open about six inches. At least, he hadn't noticed it before. It invited him to examine its contents. He walked over and slid it open all the way. He stood there mouth agape with eyes uncontrollably blinking. There were only a few bare hangers! *No clothes? What the hell is happening?* He sat down hard on the dumfounded bed confused and disoriented. "No clothes? No clothes?" he repeated to himself aloud, shaking his head in bewilderment. "How can there be no clothes?" he asked, as though expecting an answer. There was no reply. The force of the desperate question escaped the room and then the house and headed out to eventually fill the universe. Even the universe was silent on the matter.

Algernon sauntered into the room investigating the ruckus, sat in the middle of the room, and stared at his clueless competition. Karl Otto slowly shook his head trying to relieve himself of the panic ignited by his confusion. "What could have happened? We had such a great time last night!" He buried his head in his frustrated and confused palms. "Why would she leave? For that matter, how could she have taken all of her belongings without me hearing her in the space of less than four hours? Did she pack everything up and put it all in the car before I got home last night? If she planned to leave, why would she have been so uncharacteristically loving and accommodating sexually last night? Why did she sound so loving? So happy to see me? Was all of that a compensatory goodbye gesture?"

He sat on the silent bed, their bed, the bed where they had been having wild and fantastic sex just a few hours ago. The bed that had cradled them together nearly every night for over twenty-five years. He sat there feeling stunned for a very long time, a rigid statue. He didn't know how long the eternal blankness lasted before he stirred.

"What is happening?" he heard himself ask aloud to his image reflected in Grace's vanity mirror sitting stoically across from him. He made a gesture of helpless inquiry, but there was no answer forthcoming; just the shaking of the reflective head that mimicked his own. But oddly, the meaning seemed subtly incongruous. It was the same movement, except left-handed. It was less like his own "I don't know" and more like "Don't ask."

He didn't notice Algernon climbing onto the bed and nestling up to him. He stared at his reflection for a minute longer feeling numb and blank. The entire world had come to a momentary halt before he felt the Earth begin to rotate again.

He went to the garage and Grace's car was gone. He lifted his shoulders in disbelief and unconsciously spread his hands wide in total confusion and helplessness. It was as if they were saying, "What the hell is this?" He dropped his arms abruptly and his shoulders slouched in surrender to his confusion. "How is this even possible? It has been over three and a half hours, maybe four, since I sat down in that chair to write!"

Everything in his life felt out of control and, worst of all, he didn't know what he was doing. Didn't he write grief on the pad without knowing it? It frightened him to think that he didn't always have conscious control over what he did. There seemed to be forces outside of his conscious awareness at work. "And, speaking of not being in control of things, where is the least controllable thing in my life? Grace. Well. Next to the cat."

He sat dumbstruck for what felt like a lifetime. Flashback memories of his life with Grace engulfed his grey matter, seeped into the white, and permeated his whole existence. His head was vibrating and his vision blurred under a furrowed brow. Standing on the confused precipice of time peering out over the vista of the past, he swooned. He silently struggled to regain his balance... His sanity. If he had any left. He sat in a heap of sad defeat. "I have to wake up. I need some coffee. Maybe I'm caught in a dream."

He went to the kitchen, put a pod in the coffee maker, and retrieved a mug from the dishwasher. He rummaged mindlessly through the pile of mail and random papers that had accumulated on the kitchen counter, calling him and trying to distract him. It was where Grace usually left it. She almost never looked through it. She mostly left that inglorious task for him. She seemed to treat the stuff as objects of no consequence despite the necessary bills that screamed out like the carnivorous plant in The Little Shop of Horrors, "Feed me! Feed me!" demanding payment of his life's blood. Apparently she did hear the occasional shout of the ads, though. That is, if one fell out or was larger than the rest of the mail.

There were several bills intermixed with various advertisements. There was an envelope from an insurance company and another from a funeral home. He tore them open. The one from the insurance company read:

> We are in receipt of your letter notifying us of your wife Grace Otto's untimely passing. In order to complete your request, an original death certificate and the police report must be received. The original documents will be returned to you within a week of receipt.

The funeral home letter stated that Grace had been cremated and they awaited his instructions whether to FedEx the ashes to him or would he prefer to pick them up in person. There was also a bill for the "procedure" along with their condolences for his loss on an obvious a form letter preprinted on the company's letterhead.

"What's this? Grace died? She's dead? I just had sex with her last night and we had a great talk."

Another envelope had the death certificate in it. Finally, there was an envelope from the police department that contained the police report. The cover letter simply stated, "Please find enclosed the police report you requested." It said that Grace had died in a car crash months ago! "Just the facts mam!" He muttered to the envelope. The envelope offered no response except for the teardrop that moistened one small spot on the envelope.

Karl Otto felt confused and overwhelmed. He didn't have the energy to read on. He slammed the mail down on the unforgiving counter. He felt drained and fatigued. He noticed that his legs were quivering. He steadied himself on the counter. "Was I asleep for over three hours... or was I asleep for months?"

He abandoned his coffee. He felt emotionally exhausted and decided to lie down. But he didn't want to lay in their bed. He headed for the couch, leaving a trail of confused sorrow in his wake. His entire weight landed on the unsuspecting couch. A seismic tremor of magnitude ten shook the structure and objects began to fall from the shelves in his mind. His brain hurt from the aftershocks. He was too dazed to cry or accept that Grace was not only gone, but dead! He had anticipated her loss through a divorce, but not this!

"How could I forget that she is gone? Dead? There had to have been a funeral or a memorial and letters and phone calls to the insurance company, friends and family, and her work place and who knows what else." Both of their parents were gone and there would have been only the kids and friends there.

There was that music again. It surrounded him. He was infused with the all-consuming sleep. His last thought was, *I've got to check that noise. Is it the furnace or the radio alarm?*

CHAPTER FIVE
Jeremy Therapy Two:
John Doe Relaxing

The therapist mindlessly asked whether John Doe had remembered anything. "How is the search for memories going John?" He asked this without realizing that this line of inquiry had the effect of putting a thumb over the end of a running hose that created an intense back pressure of anxiety.

"I've had no progress yet." John Doe replied a little more nervous than when he sat down.

During the third session, Jeremy Lincoln said, "we've been spending our time together recounting as much as you can remember since you were hit on the head. It appears that we have gleaned all we can so far. With your permission, let's try some techniques that might help."

"Okay, what do you have in mind, Doc?"

"There are some imagery techniques along with relaxation that may assist you."

"Okay. Let's try it. I'm eager to get started." John Doe heard himself and realized that he sounded almost too eager, but he wanted to appear enthusiastic and ready to work hard. He realized that he was sitting on the edge of his chair. *Maybe, that's why the front of the chairs are so anxiously worn down.*

"Please understand," Jeremy Lincoln cautioned, "this may take some time. Be careful not to expect too much too soon. It may not be an overnight success. We need to go slowly."

John Doe felt Jeremy's hand squeezing his heart after he thrust that commitment into his chest. He had hoped the process would not be so involved and lengthy. "Slow you say Doc?"

"Since there's no brain damage, we have to assume that your amnesia is caused by psychological trauma more than the actual blow to your head. It's a little like planting a seed in the garden."

"A seed in a garden Doc?"

"Well, you can plant a seed and you can nurture it with the proper amount of soil for it to germinate and take root. You can give it the proper amount of water and light for its growth. In other words, you can create an environment that will encourage it to grow, but you can't make it grow faster by giving it too much water and light. Nor can you get it to grow if you fertilize it too much. You can't, for that matter, grab the first shoots and try to force them to grow by stretching them up. You'd pull them up and kill the plant. Nature resists being forced against its will."

John Doe was puzzled and getting tired of the long explanations and wanted to get on with it.

"There's a reason you forgot," said Jeremy. "It's a psychological block. So you may be unconsciously afraid to recall it all at once. The theory is that it may be too overwhelming. So, if we move too fast, it could actually set you back."

John Doe felt the force of a blow to his expectations as though he had been slapped across the face. *How long can this take?* "I see Doc. I'll try not to go too fast, but I don't want to move too slowly, either."

"Alright," said Jeremy, "are you comfortable sitting there in that position for a while?"

"Yes, I think so." He adjusted his legs a bit, uncrossing them into a more comfortable position. He felt the comfort of his feet supported by terra firma. The Earth seemed to be a solid pedestal, a launch pad for his blast into the past, but the disappointed vehicle was under construction. Liftoff had to wait.

"Okay, just take a deep breath and relax as much as possible. Just sit there and become aware of your breath."

John Doe did as he was bade. He had to admit that he did start to feel more comfortable.

"Alright. Now close your eyes and become aware of your feet until you really feel them. Just sit with that awareness for a few minutes."

John Doe felt the infusion of deepening pleasantness like a spring day that smelled of the dampness of hope for a newly refreshed beginning.

"After you are fully feeling your feet, inhale deeply and slowly. Then please tense the muscles in your feet and relax them as you slowly exhale. Please signal me by lifting a finger when you have accomplished this." Jeremy waited for the muscles in his patient's feet to relax and his finger to lift. His mind started to wander and he had to redirect himself back to the task at hand.

John Doe felt even more grounded when he felt his finger lifting. *Did I lift it or did it rise on its own?* He was puzzled.

"That's right. Good. Now we are going to do the same thing with each group of muscles. So, breathe in deeply while you let yourself become aware of your calf muscles and then, when you are fully aware, tighten them, inhale deeply, and then relax them as you exhale."

John Doe's muscles and breath did as they were asked.

John Doe felt the whitecaps settle and the rapids of calm return. His brain dumped the cortisol stress hormone and he felt the tides of the loving kindness of oxytocin rising and flooding his body. They continued the exercise repeating the same process with each muscle group until all had been dealt with and until John Doe seemed flaccidly relaxed. He was simply noticing the thoughts and feelings arise and fall away.

"How does that feel?"

"I feel much more relaxed and comfortable."

"That's right. You feel more relaxed and comfortable. Good." Jeremy's voice sounded pleased.

This took the bulk of the therapy visit. "So, do you think you could tell me in more detail what your experience was during this exercise?"

"Well Doc, I felt more and more relaxed and, once I was comfortable, I felt as though I was sinking deep into a place of warm numbness, but that turned into a kind of pleasant feeling of..." he paused while he searched for the right words. "Connectedness I guess you'd say. A sort of safety in the face of the chaos. Maybe that was it."

"Chaos?"

"Yeah. The chaotic chattering of my overworked mind." Another thoughtful pause. "Then I had an image come to mind. I started to see myself walking down a road."

"Oh. You had an image? You were walking down a road?"

"Yeah."

Jeremy tried not to reveal his alarm. He worried that John Doe was already jumping the gun and leaving the starting line ahead of the signal. He tried to maintain his composure. "How did you feel while you were walking?"

"I felt okay, but I got a little nervous like there was something that was going to happen, but I remembered your voice guiding me back to focus on relaxing my muscles and breathing and just observing whatever came to mind."

"Wow," said Jeremy. "We weren't going to add imagery yet. You already started taking another step." He was trying to be supportive without condoning the pace. Jeremy hesitated before he continued. He was fishing for the next thing to say. "I think it's interesting that you were able to do that. It demonstrates that you can do the work we're embarking on but I'm concerned that you might be jumping ahead too soon. I'm especially worried that, if you do this too soon at home, you might have a strong reaction before you are ready and I won't be there to help you through it."

John Doe stared at Jeremy Lincoln through a tunnel of puzzled exasperation for what seemed like a long, incredulous time before his response changed to a pained expression. "Yes. In a way. It shows us that you can accomplish the next step; but, like I said before, if we go too fast, it might set you back. I remember in high school on the track team. If we started out of the blocks too fast in a distance run, we petered out and fell behind and lost the race. This is more of a jog with a steady pace than a sprint."

"But Doc, you always asked me if I remembered anything at the beginning of the session."

"Yes, but I'm simply inquiring whether you've had any spontaneous memories. That's different than trying to force it too soon. It's probably better to take one step at a time and we're not at the second step yet."

"Alright Doc. I'll try to do it your way. I guess I'm just so intent on resolving this whole thing. But Doc, do I hold back when these images come up by themselves?"

"Well..." Long pause. "I know it may happen spontaneously, but don't push it. We want to set up the conditions for a spontaneous recall. You need the techniques to manage them when they do come up. Once you have an image, just let it be there without pursuing it until it simply fades out. Just let it come and go. If you can't relax and let it go, just come back here."

"Okay Doc. whatever you say. You're the expert," he said doubtfully. But he felt frustrated that the process had to take so long.

Expert! I know more about therapy than he does, but I'm probably just as uncertain about this as he is. "Okay, now I want you to practice this relaxation technique every day. In fact do so as much as possible until our next session in two weeks. But do just the relaxation okay?"

"Okay Doc," John Doe said. A tone of disappointment trickled past his attempt to hold it in. His words didn't match his voice. "It does feel good so I'll try," he said, letting his vocalizations cover his real emotions.

Jeremy realized that his patient wasn't convinced and he picked up on the operative word "try". "It's very important that you not only try but that you follow through at least once a day. Twice is better, and of course the more you do it, like any skill, it'll become easier and you'll relax more quickly. You may get to the point that you'll eventually be able to relax without the formal technique."

"Okay Doc. I promise I'll do it as much as I can. I really want to recover those memories. I don't have much else to do anyway."

"Good. But remember that this is just the first step. Don't even try to regain memories at this point. You may not have any memories yet. If you do have spontaneous ones that's alright, but don't be discouraged if you don't. The point is, don't push yourself. Don't try to have them. That would only increase the tension and defeat the purpose. There are other things we'll do to build on this process. It'll be absolutely the best if you get to the point that it's no longer a technique, but more of a natural thing you can do. However, it'll still be very effective if you just get good at this. Letting things come to mind and letting them fade out is the important thing."

"Okay Doc." He hesitated for a minute while he thought, *okay, okay, okay!* "You know Doc, I wake up in the morning now and I'm scared for a few minutes because I don't know where I am. I finally realize that I'm in the shelter, but I still feel like I'm at the event horizon of a black hole. It's as though I'm floating in space with no up or down, just helplessly drifting toward oblivion."

"I can't imagine how scary that must be for you, but now you're learning a way to notice it and let it fade away." With that, the visit ended and John Doe disappeared out the office door and proceeded out of the clinic and caught a bus to the shelter.

Jeremy sat in his chair in the empty office. Somehow a dark and heavy weight seemed to follow his patient out of the office accompanied by the severe draft of a silent blankness in his wake. The room seemed to become emptier than before he had entered it. Much more desolate than expected.

Jeremy Lincoln started to wonder, *am I pushing John too fast?* But, he thought, *there's no putting the cat back in the bag now. Maybe it's Schrodinger's cat. It all depends on where and when you look in the bag.*

CHAPTER SIX
Karl's Grace

Karl Otto was being awakened by someone gently shaking him by the shoulder. Someone was calling him. "Karl, Karl." It was a feint female voice moving toward him from far away at first, until it picked up speed and rushed full bore into his mind. The closer it came the more it sounded like Grace. Adrenalin rushed into his system, his eyes popped open and his head whipped around painfully on his stiff neck. It was Grace! He rubbed the remaining sand of sleep out of his eyes and looked again. It *was* her!

"Grace!" he blurted out. He grabbed her and pulled her to him.

"Of course silly," she said, gasping for air through his rib-crushing grip that constricted her breathing. "Who did you think it was? One of your other girlfriends?" she croaked. Then she squeezed out, "you're killing me with kindness!"

"Oh God!" He loosened the constriction. "I'm sorry. Are you alright. You know I'd never purposely hurt you," he said. "I was disoriented for a second." He looked away. "I was having a nightmare. It was so intense!"

She looked puzzled while taking a deep restorative breath trying not to faint from lack of oxygen. "What are you doing out here on the couch? I woke up and wanted to snuggle, but you were gone," she gasped, "I missed you! I got a little scared when you weren't there. What are you doing on the couch?"

There was a pause and he stared at her for a minute. "Scared? Why were you scared?" he asked.

She tried to sidestep the question. "Didn't you enjoy last night?" She was pretending to pout now.

"Oh I loved it!" he said, "It's just that I was so stimulated that I woke up and couldn't get back to sleep. I didn't want to disturb you. You were sleeping so soundly that you didn't even know I kissed you. So I got up and had something to eat and I lay on the couch. I had a beer and I turned on the stream, but there was nothing on it that was worth wasting my time on. I must have fallen asleep. Sorry."

"So, I drove you to drink?" she joked.

"No... I..." Then he realized it was her attempt at humor. In the past, he had been so ready for her criticism that he had reacted without thinking like a whipped dog until he realized that he was reacting automatically. He got up and slowly stretched a bit. He yawned. "Shall I come back to bed? What time is it?" he inquired.

"No. I'm no longer in the mood and I'm wide awake." She pretended to pout again with her lower lip prominently distended. There was a lilt in her voice as a smile lit her face. "Besides, we both have to get ready for work." She didn't seem upset. Her words were matter of fact in tone. There seemed to be an air of relief in her voice and she was smiling early in the morning after just getting out of bed. This was unlike the Grace he knew.

There's another surprise. It seemed to Karl Otto that Grace's grumpy gremlins had disappeared down the drain of sanity to be swallowed and cleansed in the ocean of lucid love.

"What was your nightmare about?" Grace inquired, looking over her shoulder on the way into the kitchen.

"Oh, I don't remember now," he lied with a dismissive flourish of his right hand. "You know how it is. You forget it after you wake up. You're aware of the nightmare, but you can't remember the content. You just know you had it and maybe there's a residual feeling." He realized that he was over-explaining in his attempt to hide his real feelings. He didn't want to ruin what they had started last night.

"Well, I'd like to hear about it if you remember."

"Okay, I'll try to remember."

"I hope you will. I love that kind of thing."

He took a puzzled double-take. His face wrinkled into a big metaphorical question mark. "Since when?" He stumbled into the kitchen after her. The cat scampered ahead of him. Algernon always seemed to be competing with him for the favor of her attention, love, and physical closeness. Come to think of it, both of them always seemed to be following her around like a dog in heat.

"Since just about forever. Didn't I ever tell you?" she said.

"No. I don't remember you ever saying that."

She slipped a pod into the coffee machine. "Want one?"

"Huh? A nightmare?"

"No, dummy. A cup of coffee. Do you want one?"

"Oh... Sorry. I guess I'm still a little dazed from sleep. Yeah. Sure. Coffee would be great. Thank you."

Karl Otto was on another planet ensconced in thought. He was trying to grasp what had happened. *Did I have a dream that Grace was dead? It seemed so real.* He wanted to ask her about last night, but somehow he knew beyond any doubt that it would ruin everything if he told her he had such a vivid dream of her demise. *Not a romantic notion, especially after such a great evening.* He was certain that she would take his inquiry the wrong way. He didn't want to seem to be questioning the tremendous step forward they had taken. It was simply a nightmare. *But I remember lying down on the couch, didn't I?* His head was drowning in impossible questions.

Grace took her coffee into the bedroom, trailed by the cat. Karl Otto grabbed the cat food and dished it out, but Algernon didn't come. Karl Otto shrugged with a sigh. He sat at the kitchen table feeling more puzzled than ever. He slowly stood up, scratched his head, and mumbled, "I must have dreamt the whole thing! Weird." He wondered if he had thought that or if he said it aloud; Just as Grace reappeared. When Grace came back into the kitchen, she was a vision of splendor, overdressed for work.

Grace held her left earlobe to insert an earring. She was five feet seven inches tall. She had kept her figure and her clothes always looked good on her. In fact, Karl couldn't remember her ever wearing anything that detracted from her beauty. She had on a light blue blouse under a dark blue blazer with a matching skirt. Her sheer stockings enhanced her slender legs and her shoes were black pumps that made her five feet nine. There was a scarf around her neck that had a red and blue design with a white swirl that wove in and out. Her pearl necklace and the matching earrings that hung down on her long beautifully smooth neck beaconing him to kiss it, completed the ensemble. She had long black hair tied back with a clip.

"Wow! You look gorgeous! Which boyfriend did you dress up for today?" he joked.

"Ha, ha, ha." She faked a laugh and reached over to lightly stroke his cheek. "You're the only blind man for me babe! We can look into a seeing-eye dog later. I saw an ad with a phone number. Or maybe a white cane." She smiled and kissed him on the forehead. "But aren't you going to get dressed for work? You'll be late."

He pondered this for a minute sailing off in thought with a wrinkled brow before he spoke in a thoughtfully slow tone. "No. I think I'll call in and work from home today. All I have to do is make phone calls and emails and write some reports today," he lied. "No internal company meetings and no sorties with clients today." He wanted to stay home and he didn't want to do much work today. *Well, maybe I'll do some later... Maybe.*

"Okay. Well, I'll see you later." She hugged him, kissed him on the forehead and then planted a big prolonged one on his lips and turned to leave. She took about three steps and stopped. She turned around and fixed a serious gaze on Karl Otto. "I love you, you know?"

"I love you too babe, very much." He flashed her a huge grin. "And you still are a babe," he added with a flourish of his right arm.

She turned and waved over her shoulder, jangling her bracelets. "See you later liar, if you're not consumed by your pants on fire! Bye." She bent down to pet Algernon and pushed him back from the door.

He watched her slip out the door about to be swallowed up by her world. The door closed on his universe. *This is starting to feel like a badly edited movie that had all the scenes spliced together in the wrong order.* He couldn't follow the plot.

The cat looked at him, flicked his tail, and defiantly ate his fill as if to say, "I'm only eating this because I'm hungry. Not because you dished it out!" Then he slunk toward the basement stairs. He stopped and crouched on the landing as though he were stalking something invisible. His hind quarters vibrated as if he was gathering energy. It reminded Karl Otto of the dragsters revving in anticipation of the starting flag at the strip where he used to go when he was a teenager.

Vroom, vroom, he said to himself.

Algernon was poised at the starting line and suddenly shot down the stairs with a burst of power chasing after his hallucination.

Karl Otto stood and walked over to the counter. He rummaged through the mail. There were no letters from the police or the funeral home. No insurance letter. *Just a dream. Maybe a dream within a dream?*

Karl Otto walked into the living room and lay back on the couch. He was drowsy. The over-use of his brain's energy in rumination and worry made him tired. Even watching the cat had tired him out. Besides, he reckoned that he had slept very little last night.

CHAPTER SEVEN
Jeremy Therapy Three: Deepening

The next therapy session was devoted to checking on John Doe's relaxation technique. Jeremy asked John Doe to demonstrate his procedure. He took a few minutes to do so while Jeremy waited and tried to keep his attention from wandering from the room. Jeremy could see that his charge was doing well and that he was able to enter the relaxed state much more quickly. It seemed effortless, too.

There was a slight unconscious flicker of John Doe's eyelids. He tensed and relaxed each muscle group easily and he appeared to be loose and relaxed. His muscles seemed flaccid. Jeremy watched as John Doe seemed to melt before him. For a second, he thought he saw his patient shimmer slightly, but he thought that was just a trick of the lighting in the room.

"You're doing well with this part of it. How much time have you spent practicing this?"

"I've done it about three times a day."

"Well, you've done very well with it." Jeremy thought about the past patients who claimed they forgot to practice at home or who didn't fully understand the instructions. Sometimes it seemed that they immediately forgot the exercise as soon as they left the office. They had stripped off a cloak of some sort and invisibly and left everything there in the office. *Whatever happens in the therapy office stays in the therapy office*, he mused with an ironic smirk. But John Doe was a virtuoso compared to them. *Impressive,* he thought.

"Now, John, we're going to add a small step. You need to remain relaxed whenever you have a memory whether it is a comfortable one or not. So I don't want you to go back into your memories too far just yet. Don't try to go back to that trauma in the street yet. Just go back to a pleasant time. It might be a day or a week or even a month ago, but don't go too far yet."

John Doe imagined a magic portal of some kind leading to the past. Maybe a wormhole through space-time he had seen in sci-fi movies.

"So, after you get relaxed," Jeremy continued, "I want you to travel back in your memory to that time of your choice. But I want you to remain relaxed the entire time. If you begin to tense up, then stop and relax again or, if it's too difficult to relax, drop it and come back to here and now. The key is to remain comfortable or regain that relaxation and focus if you become distracted. We don't want to reinforce any tension while you're in a memory. Remember, any thoughts or images, pleasant or not, that come up, just note them and let them drift away naturally."

John Doe wasn't listening any more, but pretended he was. "Okay Doc. It sounds doable."

"Don't forget, if you feel you're getting upset and you can't relax, you can just come out of it."

"Sure thing, Doc." John Doe sounded disappointed, but willing to go along with the program... for now.

"Alright," said Jeremy Lincoln. "Let's try it. I'll wait while you get relaxed and go back a ways into a memory. When you come back you can tell me about it. If we're running out of time, I'll let you know. I'll leave enough time for a debriefing."

Jeremy sat quietly watching while John Doe worked his way through the exercise. He thought about his story and about how it must feel to be completely blank before a certain point in one's life. He imagined how scary it must be. He respected John Doe's drive to recover his past, too. He was one of the most motivated patients, or consumers, as the community mental health agency liked to call them.

When there was about ten minutes left in the session, Jeremy interrupted him. "John, it's time to come back," he said quietly, so not to startle him.

John Doe took a few minutes to return from his reverie and rubbed his eyes.

The therapist asked, "Can you tell me about what you experienced?"

"I remembered an incident at the shelter two days ago when a man came up to me and wanted to take my blanket. I said no, but he insisted. He reached for it, but I blocked his progress. I found myself unconsciously placing myself between him and the blanket. I saw one of the staff walking by and signaled him for assistance. He was able to redirect the man and told him that he would be asked to leave if he didn't behave himself. He settled down and went away. I think the guy is mentally ill."

"Did you feel upset while you were remembering it?"

"I did notice that I started to feel tension creeping in during that memory, but I took your advice and relaxed. I tried to focus on my relaxation and my breath and let it fade away. I think I was at least partly successful."

"Good," said Jeremy. "Sometimes it's best to view the memories as if you were watching them happen somewhere else, like you're a spectator rather than a participant. Like in the third person." Jeremy realized that John Doe had gone farther than he had been asked to. Jeremy realized that he had forgotten to tell him to retrieve a positive or benign memory. But this one seemed to end well enough, he thought... *I guess.*

"Yeah, I see what you mean. I guess I did that in a way, I was able to relax and pull out of it. I refocused and relaxed. When I went back to it, I no longer felt like I was absorbed in it. I was kind of a witness. A voyeur peeking into my own memory. Maybe it's like Charles Dickens' *A Christmas Carol* when Scrooge visits the past and future to observe himself, but no one can see him. He's just observing the scene." He paused while he thought about it. "I think I felt better because I relaxed, but also because I felt free to climb out of that deep well if I wanted to. I wasn't stuck in the emotional experience of it with no escape."

"That's great! Good insight, John." The session ended on that positive note and the room became lighter. Both therapist and patient felt a weight beginning to lift. John Doe said goodbye and Jeremy responded in kind. He left the building and walked to the bus stop.

Jeremy was impressed with the progress so far. *This guy, whatever his real name is, continues to amaze me with his abilities and his persistence. I think if anyone has a chance of recalling a dissociated traumatic memory, it's John Doe.*

CHAPTER EIGHT
Curious George

John Doe stepped onto the bus and swiped the bus pass across the reader. He was given a bus card for transportation to and from the shelter and a card they used to call food stamps for buying groceries and household items. The truth was that many of these cards were sold on the streets to others for cash in the quest for alcohol and drugs or other things that were not on the approved list. The driver had a cloth name tag sewn to the lapel of his uniform that said GEORGE. George said, "Hi!" in a cheerful voice.

John Doe said, "Hi," and sat in the seat behind the driver.

George said, "You've been on my bus before, haven't you?"

"I guess so. I've taken this bus for a couple weeks now. Yes."

"I'm George."

"John D..." He hesitated. He decided not to say 'John Doe' and left it at John.

"Glad to meet you John D."

"No. It's just John."

"Oh. Sorry, John." George was a large man with hands like Easter hams. He was a muscular man of probably about six feet three or four inches tall. He had a friendly face, but there was an air about him that suggested you should remain on his good side.

Don't cross this guy, thought John Doe.

"Nice to meet you," George said. "Are you gonna take this bus often?"

"Yeah. I guess so. Probably... Maybe."

George's personal policy was that of getting to know all of his regulars as much as possible through friendly conversation and observation. He was almost psychic in his uncanny visions of people. This assisted him to spot anyone who might cause trouble and determine who he could rely on if he needed support with an unruly passenger. He wanted to be friendly and tried to engage everyone in the hopes that they would do as he asked, especially if there was an emergency. He also wanted passengers to know that he didn't want any trouble, but if they gave him any, he could give back in kind.

George had been doing this job a long time and he had witnessed more strange things in one week than most people witness in a lifetime. If people liked him and felt safe with him, he reckoned they would more than likely be cooperative. Even the crazy ones, and there were plenty of those. He could size up a new passenger almost before they stepped onto the bus and certainly before they sat down. He watched for facial expressions, body language and he noticed whether they spoke to him and their tone of voice when they did. Even the way they handled their bus card or however they paid, was scrutinized.

"Are you staying at the shelter or do you work there?" he inquired of this new passenger.

John Doe realized later that this driver noticed when and where people boarded as part of his analysis.

"No. I sleep there. I'm between jobs at the moment."

George thought, *between jobs? This guy doesn't fit this scene. He has to be in a deep pile of road apples. He must have slipped at least a couple rankings down the pecking order.* He said, "What did you do before?"

John Doe felt ambushed. He hesitated before he answered. His hesitation did not go unnoticed. "I'd have to kill you if I told you," he laughed.

George saw that he was not ready to reveal too much and felt him pull back into the sacred shadows of anonymity. His hesitation made the driver feel more suspicious, but he chalked it up to embarrassment... *For now. John, if that's his real name, seems to be much more educated and sophisticated than the average passenger I've encountered. I reckon John has encountered some kind of major setback that made him homeless, at least temporarily. I've seen it before. Usually, they are white collar criminals who had lost everything and had served time or were facing that fate. But John seems different somehow. He doesn't act like the others. He's too relaxed and congenial. He didn't have the hard edge of an ex-con and he wasn't as tense and aloof like those facing charges.* John Doe was memorable. He didn't belong out there on the streets and yet there he was. It seemed to George that he was vulnerable and probably naive about how to handle himself in that environment. George felt protective. "Here you are," he said. "It's your stop."

John Doe said, "Thanks, George. Glad to meet you sir. See you later."

"See you, John." George noted that John had addressed him with the formal "sir."

As he exited the bus, John Doe thought about the bus driver. *He's something of a practical psychologist in a way. A natural. He sizes people up based upon their behavior and develops a relationship with them on his own terms. He is able to build rapport with them. He also has strategies to manage their thoughts and feelings as well as their behaviors. Entering his bus is like stepping out of their usual experience into another world. Their frame of reference shifts. I feel it too.*

It's too bad, he thought, *that George didn't go to college and work in the human service community. But in a way, he's doing a lot of good in his current role. Besides, college might have ruined his skills by distracting him with things that were too academic.* He liked the old guy. He guessed just about everyone did.

CHAPTER NINE
Karl Otto's Homework

Karl Otto woke up feeling groggy. He had stayed home ostensibly to do his work remotely, but his heart just wasn't in it. He tried to open the computer and dictate a report, but he remembered that there were signed documents at the office and he couldn't complete the reports without them. "Shit!" he blurted out. "All of the stuff I need is on my desk at the office!"

He couldn't remember how to patch in remotely, either. The instructions and the special passwords were locked in his desk. He didn't usually work from home. He only brought the passwords home when he anticipated doing so or when he was out of town. The passwords had to be changed every month for security and he couldn't remember them all because they had to be long strings of nonsense with numbers, capital and lower-case letters, symbols, etc.

"Damn!" he said halfheartedly. He gave up, but he wasn't all that disappointed. He didn't really want to work, anyway. He was too distracted. Karl Otto sighed and sat down in the living room to rest and think. "I'm glad to have Grace back even though I don't understand it." He said this as if he was talking to some absent person. He caught himself thinking the dream was real. At least it did seem real.

He got up and went into the kitchen and looked through the mail. The death certificates, the police report and the cremation letter were there. "What the hell?" He thought back over last night. Grace had been very different. *It had to be a dream didn't it?* He paused, suspended in confusion, then he dragged himself over and sat down dead weight on the surprised kitchen chair. "Now it's real? At first it's real, then in isn't, then it is. What the hell?" He shook his head. His thoughts were oscillating with increasing rapidity. He wondered if his head would vibrate off of his shoulders. He thought he remembered this happen in the movies sometimes. *It was real. No, it had to be a dream.* The fog lifted, but it was replaced by a cloudy sky that blocked the light of understanding. *But it felt so real. But it can't be real... I must be going out of my mind.*

Why would I have had a dream like that if she's dead? But we had such a wonderful night. Everything seems to be changing between Grace and me but was this morning a dream too? Karl Otto stared out into the void. He didn't see anything. The breaks suddenly caught and all of his thoughts came to a screeching halt so suddenly that he slammed into himself. The concussion made him simply stare in numb silence. Nothing even crossed his mind for what seemed like hours. A neon sign in his head slowly flashed on and off, "yes, no, yes, no..."

Algernon had crawled onto his lap and was being mindlessly petted. Very unsatisfying. Eventually, the cat tired of it and unceremoniously jumped down and went for the food dish. Apparently, a more acceptable alternative. Karl Otto just shook his head. It weighed a ton. It dropped to his chest. Algernon had nothing better to do and returned, like it or not, to the only distracted lap available at the moment. At least he could get his ears scratched. A tertiary choice at best, on his list of priorities. That is, if a cat has priorities or even a list, for that matter.

Karl Otto took out his phone. It weighed a ton. He dialed his office still mindlessly scratching the cat's ears. The receptionist answered sounding like she had a clamp on her nose. "Hi. This is Karl Otto. Please put me through to Ed Johnson. Thanks."

After three minutes of unmemorable Muzak a voice said, "This is Ed." The voice was so loud and clear that Karl Otto had to pull the phone away from his ear. He looked around as if Ed was right there in the room.

"Ed. This is Karl Otto. I think I'll try to get some work done here at home. I'm not feeling well today."

"Okay Karl, but I need that Ibsen account info soon okay? I understand all that has happened to you recently Karl, but at some point you've got to get back in the groove. It's been several months now." He hesitated awkwardly. "You've been under the weather quite a lot since..." He was still avoiding the topic of Grace's death. "You know." The world paused for a moment whilst the topic changed. "Karl, I've backed off on you lately, but I can't keep covering for you much longer. You've always been my best worker Karl. I need you back in form."

"Okay, Ed. I'll try to get back in the groove."

"Okay Karl, but I do need that Ibsen stuff soon."

"Alright. I'll come in tomorrow if I'm feeling better."

"I hope you feel better soon. Take care of yourself. I didn't want to say this to you, but I have pressure from above. Bye, Karl."

He hung up. Ed didn't sound angry, but he was worried and irritated. The pressure was getting to him too. *Geez! I've been slacking off? That's not like me. And he said it's been months now! And...* He thought for a minute. *The only thing that could have been effecting me would have been if Grace really died.* He abruptly hoisted himself to his feet, unceremoniously dumping the cat onto the floor. Algernon did not appreciate it and thrust a hiss along with a characteristically dissatisfied flick of his tail at him.

Karl Otto stood there wavering back and forth as if he was going to do one thing and then changed his mind and was going to do another, but without any actual plan or direction. His mind was lost and he couldn't find it, even though he grabbed his head to stop the spinning. He couldn't decide what to do or where to go. He sat down again in a heap. He didn't notice that it was the world that was going in circles. *Maybe I need to see a shrink. Maybe I'm going crazy. Maybe I wasn't dreaming. Maybe I was hallucinating. Or would it be more appropriate to see a shaman, under the circumstances?* He sat up straight as another possibility popped into his mind. *What if it's really happening? What if I'm not insane and something bizarre is happening around me?* He paused for a gigantic yawn. *If that's true, how would I know whether it's me being bizarre or the world around me is weird?* Pause. *Maybe both? I guess every crazy person thinks his perceptions and beliefs are correct and everyone else misperceives reality.*

He bent forward and planted his elbows on his knees. He grabbed his head with both hands and squeezed tight trying to prevent the escape of any more drops of rationality. He heard a low guttural scream coming from somewhere and soon realized it was coming from previously unexplored territory deep in his own gut. *RRRRRRRRRRRRRRRRRRRRRRRRRRRRRRRRR!* The cat beat it, jet-propelled, to his dark basement underworld. Karl Otto could feel his head ready to explode. It was as though it would blow apart if his hands didn't hold it together. *Oh my God. I'm losing it!*

He stood up again and flew to the living room and came to a crash landing on the couch. He grabbed the remote and turned on the news stream hoping it would distract him with at least a few minutes of relief. He needed an escape. *Maybe I can at least distract myself for a while with some gibberish.*

The midday news was on. The news reader was speaking. "There was a bombing in Lebanon today and seven people were killed and thirty-five were seriously injured. Authorities are blaming terrorists and a representative of the government stated that they are doing all they can to find the perpetrators and bring them to justice." *Just what I need. More bad news!*

He changed the channel. A local story about Valentine's Day came into view. The female reporter began talking about all the possible inexpensive gifts available for Valentine's Day, February fourteenth in two days! "Wait a minute! Yesterday was November third!" He sat up abruptly in numb silence. "Did I actually lose more than three months?!" He was addressing the screen under his breath while slowly shaking his head. The reporter continued on as though she had ignored his question. He instantly felt alone and adrift in an unknown space.

He shut off the stream and looked at his wrist watch. It registered February twelfth! Now Karl Otto was desperate. He started pacing around frantically. "Oh my God, Oh my God, Oh - my - God!" He repeated precisely nine times. "This is crazy!!" He stood up and before he knew what he was doing, he started pacing. "I missed Thanksgiving and Christmas as well as New Years? I missed the Super Bowl party at Jeff's that we attend every year. Oh, my Go-d!" He placed heavy emphasis on the "d" in God. His pacing accelerated. It was as if Karl Otto was revving up for takeoff. He exhausted himself with the expenditure of his manic physical and psychic energy.

He felt depleted, completely spent emotionally. He came in on automatic pilot for a landing, but this time on the bed as he drifted into the arms of Morpheus he thought he heard the sound of the Lyre. His last thought was, *is it the furnace or is there music coming from next door?*

The Juxtaposition Paradox Charles R. Stern

CHAPTER TEN
George on My Mind

John Doe dragged himself out of his therapy session again after little progress and mounting disappointment. He boarded the bus and sat in his usual seat behind George. "Hi George," he said in a shrugging monotone.

"Hi, John. Where to today sir?" he joked with a smile.

"Home George!" he said with a reciprocal smile, sounding as if George was a limo driver.

"Yes sir!" said George. "I hope you don't mind if we stop and pick up a few friends on the way."

"Not at all George. The more, the merrier. Carry on!" The banter with George always seemed to cheer him up. He realized a grin had begun to permeate his face.

The bus picked up a few more riders. John Doe watched the passengers boarding and he observed George's acute abilities to scrutinize them. George always smiled no matter how rude the customer was, but he was always firm with them. He was the master of authority mixed with empathetic assertiveness. "I'm sorry if you're having a hard time," he'd say, "but I can't give you a free ride. I'm monitored by the company and I'd be fired." The individual would protest that they desperately needed to get somewhere but didn't have enough money. He'd repeat and add, "I'm so sorry, but I can't risk my job in such hard times. You understand."

He would don a sympathetic facial expression along with a sheepish brow wrinkling and pleading of hands in a hunched shouldered posture. He was actually eliciting that person's unconscious empathy for *him*! After all, George could lose his job whereas the passenger was merely inconvenienced. The person, John Doe realized, would be gored on the horns of their own dilemma. In a deep quandary, they would stand there stunned not knowing what to say.

They were obviously not prepared for anyone to turn them down without derision. He had given them no excuse to argue or plead. One man actually turned in a circle twice silently opening and closing his mouth in confusion whether to exit the bus or argue with George. Most of them would miraculously find an extra crumpled bill or handful of coins in his pocket or her purse. Sometimes, they protested that they must have left their bus pass at home, but rummage around playing the game of purse until, "Oh! Here it is!" Otherwise, they would exit the bus appearing confused; probably more because they couldn't figure out how they ended up having more sympathy for George than he showed them.

George would occasionally whisper a comment to John Doe pointing out a certain passenger's potential for making trouble or the fact that they had done so in the past. He also commented, for example, on the little elderly lady who always took his bus on Thursdays to and from her daughter's apartment across town. She was so bent over with osteoporosis and scoliosis that all she could see was her own shuffling feet. She was short to begin with, and the devastation of osteoporosis had shrunk her considerably. So much so, that she could barely manage the steps to enter the bus.

George would pull up to the curb as close as possible so she had a smaller step, but this was not enough. He always felt obliged to help her up. He wondered why her daughter didn't come to see her at her own apartment. He thought the daughter must be unfeeling or maybe she was more disabled than the old lady. He clearly felt sorry for her.

He had many stories to tell. It occurred to John Doe that George might be just a little too observant and intuitive. The bus pulled up at the shelter. "Your stop sir," George joked.

"Thank you, George. Carry on."

"Yes, sir!" They both laughed.

It's a good thing that George takes this all in fun and that he doesn't take offense, he thought. *But then, maybe he read my personality in the same way he read all the other passengers and figured this kind of banter would make me a comfortable ally. It's a bit scary. I wonder if he knows more about me than I'd like... or more than I know about myself!*

The bus pulled away and George watched after John Doe through the side mirror as he entered the shelter safely. "That John," he commented to himself, the only one who cared to listen, "he really doesn't belong out there. I hope he'll be okay. He's not streetwise."

CHAPTER ELEVEN
In and Out

Karl Otto awoke when the alarm sounded. He lay there not wanting to spend the effort of rolling over to hit the snooze. But the snooze was being hit and the buzzing ceased. This woke him up more than any buzzer could have. The cat walked over him and fled the room. He was certain the cat had accidently stepped on the snooze button. His eyes closed. *It had to be an accident. Algernon's not smart enough to have learned to do it on purpose*, he thought. He paused, thinking about the possibility that the cat... *No, Not possible!* He symbolically shook his head. Karl Otto felt a movement next to him. A chill flashed through him. In one reflexive, defensive, fearful flip, he wheeled his body around in the bed and he saw Grace next to him! "Grace!" he blurted out.

She jumped back. She had drifted back to sleep and was startled awake. "What? What's the matter? Karl?" Her body bolted up into a sitting position, but her brain lagged behind. Once she caught up to herself, her head snapped back and forth scanning the room searching for the fire or the intruder.

"Sorry. I think I must have been dreaming about you."

"About me? What was it about? Why did you yell?"

"I don't know. I just heard myself yell your name and woke myself up," he lied.

"Geez Karl! You freaked me out. I thought there was a home invasion or something!"

"I'm sorry. I'd stop if I could, but I don't know how to stop dreaming."

"I know. I know. But it's upsetting." Her voice dropped a few decibels when the remaining scales of sleep fell from her eyes and the dawn of rationality finally kicked in. She stopped herself from complaining and her forehead buckled with frown lines. "I'm sorry," Grace apologized. "I know you can't help it. You don't control dreams. I have to stop being so irritable in the morning." She sucked her lips between her teeth and stared off in deep thought, but she really didn't see anything. Her heart was still galloping so fast that she had to struggle to rein it in. She was staring through the void in her own head. It was as though her eyes suddenly turned inward as if she could peer into her own brain. She was trying to redact her irritation.

She got up and sequestered herself in the bathroom for the duration. Algernon always perched himself on the counter gazing at her reflection while she performed her rituals. He was her totem. He sat so still just staring at her image that sometimes Karl Otto wondered if Algernon was really a voyeur. Maybe he was a reincarnated human and enjoyed staring at her feminine loveliness.

He heard Grace doing God knows what women do in there. All he knew was that there were an amazing number of lotions and cosmetics that couldn't possibly be used every day. She disappeared into what seemed like a room that she mysteriously transformed into an alien landscape. *And who knows what was accumulating in there.* The number of bottles, tubes, and sundry jars and other containers was growing exponentially. Karl Otto guessed that Grace bought every new miracle beauty product that came along and abandoned the ones she had already purchased. *She probably kept the old ones in case she decided they were better and then proceeded to forget them.* She was in a never-ending struggle to stem the tide of entropy. He knew that everything was headed for dissolution, but he always thought she looked good, even without makeup and no matter what she wore on her worst days. Of course, she disagreed and thought he was joking or lying. He always grinned.

She'd point out a gray hair or a crow's feet wrinkle. He'd offer a gentle stroke to her hair or face and smile. Counter arguments, he had learned long ago, never dissuaded her.

He got up and headed for the kitchen, placed a pod into the coffee dispenser, and waited for the flow to the top off his cup. He put in another pod for Grace and walked over to the table and sat down. He took two sips before he remembered the mail. He stood and walked back over to the counter. He shuffled through the pile. He stopped and stared at it. He realized he was slumped over and stretched back up to his full height. Then he shrugged in resignation.

There was no death certificate or bill from the funeral home nor was there the police report! *It had to have been a dream, doesn't this prove it? Doesn't it?*

Grace hurried into the kitchen adjusting her bra straps and tugging at her dress. She grabbed a cup of coffee. The cat following right behind her. She said, "I have to run."

"What about breakfast?"

"I'll stop at the drive-thru and get a breakfast sandwich of some kind. I'm running behind." She kissed him on the lips and jetted out the door into her world. "Love you!" she yelled over her shoulder.

"Love you back!" he yelled after her.

He decided to stay home and pretend to work remotely again for several hours, but accomplished almost nothing save staring into space most of the time. He eventually fell asleep on the couch. Algernon crawled up next to him settling for second best or was he running in third place behind Grace and food? He had exhausted himself with worry, quandary and lack of sleep. He drifted off into a nightmare he wouldn't remember.

CHAPTER TWELVE
Jeremy Therapy Four:
Push Me Pull You

John Doe told Jeremy that he thought he was doing pretty well getting into a relaxed state between visits. He had been focusing on relaxing whenever he felt fear or anxiety coming on.

"Can you give me an example?"

"Well, Doc..." He was silent for a moment while recent recall cognition fought its way back to his conscious brain. "I was on the bus and a drunk stumbled aboard and started to harass George, the driver. I felt some fear, but I remembered to relax. I did it pretty well. I felt a kind of barrier between that guy and me."

Jeremy was a little alarmed. "I'm concerned that you tried to remain calm. I'm concerned because you shouldn't do the relaxation in the face of real danger. If you need to run away or defend yourself, you can't just sit there and get hurt."

"I understand, but I trusted George to handle it. He knew the guy and he got the man off the bus."

Jeremy Lincoln said, "Great!" Jeremy's enthusiasm began to overtake him before he knew it. "You can relax even in the proximity of such a real 'here and now' situation especially after being hit on the head like you did." He was thoughtfully silent for a minute. He seemed to be pondering the next thing to say while trying to quell his excitement. "I don't want to sound contradictory." Jeremy suddenly realized the confusion of what seemed a mixed message. You have to assess the situation. If sitting still and relaxing is dangerous, you have to run or protect yourself if attacked. Relaxation and an assessment of the situation is good when dealing with a memory or, if there's time in a real 'here and now situation', but reflexes need to come into play if you're in imminent danger. You can use the increased concentration you've been practicing, but you need to remain focused on the present danger."

"Okay, Doc. I see what you mean. I'll be more careful."

"Alright, good," said Jeremy; "now we're going to add another element. Another step, so to speak that is, if you feel up to it."

"I'm okay with it Doc. I'll do whatever will help me remember."

"Let's have you get into the relaxed, focused state you've been practicing. I'll wait. You can signal me when you're relaxed by lifting a finger to let me know. Then I'll guide you through the next step."

John Doe sat for about five minutes relaxing before he felt his finger lift.

Jeremy sat half watching, but he was immersed in his own thoughts about John Doe and the rapid progress he was making. *John is eager and intelligent and he has the time to practice. He is sincere and highly motivated. His story and reports of progress, as well as his presentation in our sessions, are all consistent. I've never seen any evidence that would make me suspect anything but a genuine effort.* Jeremy saw John Doe's finger lift.

"Okay. Good. Now I want you to go back into your past, even if it's an hour or a day. Just a memory. You can experience it and when you feel as if you have done that enough, you can come back here and now and tell me about it, if that's alright with you.

"So, keeping your eyes closed, I want you to start to move slowly back to a time before you came here today. You can go back to yesterday or a month ago or however far back you wish to go. Just let me know when you've gone as far as you want to go in your memory even if it's just an hour or a day or a month. Just let me know so I can help you with the next step. Just signal me with your finger like before."

There was a very long five-minute gap in time while he did so. Jeremy kept his gaze on John Doe's hands, but he slid back into his recursive thinking about how the other professionals would judge his performance based on John Doe's progress. If John Doe succeeded in reaching his goal, they couldn't argue with his approach. He was so lost in his defensive thoughts that he nearly missed it when the finger shot up.

"Alright. Where are you?"

"I'm in the street where I woke up bleeding with a bump on my head."

"Ah. Is that alright with you to be there?"

"Yeah, I guess."

"How do you feel being there?"

"Scared. I want to run. I'm dizzy and my vision is blurry."

"You feel like running?"

"Yes."

"Okay. Now, would it be possible to stay there for a while? You know, instead of running away?"

"I'll try, but it's scary. Someone might come back and try to hurt me again or kill me! I'm so foggy and I'm scared that I won't see him coming."

"You think it was a man who hit you?"

"I don't know. I'm just assuming it was."

"Alright, I only want you to stay as long as you feel you can for now, but remember that you're safe here and it's not happening right now. It's a memory of something that has passed. Do your focused relaxation and let the feelings fade."

"Okay. I'll try to stay longer. I'll try."

"That's great. Just let yourself do that and remember to stay as relaxed as you can like you did with me a little while ago." John Doe started to breathe deeply and appeared to relax some of his muscles. "How are you doing John?"

"Okay... I think."

"Are you still relaxed?"

"Yeah. Pretty much."

"That's good. Now I want you to become aware that this is merely a memory."

Pause.

"No matter what happens or how you feel, it's just a memory and it'll fade away. Just see it as a performance on a stage or on the stream. It's happening over there at a distance and you're just watching. You're the audience." Jeremy's voice was softer and quieter now. Precisely ten minutes dragged by before Jeremy said, "Okay John, it's time to come back now."

John Doe had been so absorbed that he was suddenly hoisted out of the past by the shock of a present he hadn't expected and propelled into a blind and uncertain future. "You're safe here with me. Please come back here when you are ready."

"Okay." John Doe continued for a minute. A tear formed in his left eye and wended its way down his cheek and caused him to sniff exactly twice. He dodged his sadness with the distraction of reality and, giving himself time to adjust, he shook himself back into the present moment.

Jeremy said, "How did that feel?"

"I was relaxed for a few seconds at first, but I got scared and felt my mind fading to black like I was going to pass out, but you helped with reminding me to relax again. I didn't relax completely, but I was able to recover and stay in the scene longer. I think I eventually got lost in the scene until you wrenched me back here." He realized that he had to explain his tear. "I started to feel sad about having my identity stolen from me."

"Do you feel alright now?"

"Yes." He lied through his foggy countenance.

"Great! Good job. I think we're making progress. But I want you to remember not to struggle with the feelings. If they become too much, just come back. Don't fight with yourself. Don't try to force yourself. Okay?"

"Okay. Should I do this between our sessions on my own?"

"If you think you'll be alright and if you don't struggle."

"Okay. I'll try."

The session powered down, ending with Jeremy watching John Doe leave. Jeremy Lincoln always had the strange sensation that John Doe vanished when he walked through the door. "Out of sight, out of mind," he said to the door. The door, in an odd way, was ominously silent as if it was withholding some secret. Jeremy shook it off and considered it a manifestation of his own insecurity.

Psychotherapy was Jeremy's world and John Doe would be out there, wherever that was, for two more weeks. Jeremy was intrigued by the whole amnesia thing and pleased that he was helping John Doe toward recovering his memories. *I hope John Doe will follow up and continue the exercise we began.* But he was realistic enough to know that most patients don't or, if they do, they only do it occasionally.

"Well," he said to the empty office, "at least we're making progress in our sessions every other week." Something in the walls seemed to respond. Was it agreement or was it simply the building settling like his grandmother always reassured herself whenever she heard a random noise in the house? While he hoped for more, he had to be careful not to push John Doe too hard.

CHAPTER THIRTEEN
Now You See It

Karl awoke two and a half hours later. There was no sign of the cat. He decided it was time he got up and really got some work done, but didn't really mean it. He arose and came to a standing position. He was painfully aware of the abrasive sandpaper in his knees, felt the stiffness in his muscles, and there was a crick in his neck. He stretched and cracked his neck in a circle. "Make a note," he dictated to the invisible secretary, "get a new couch." He rubbed his neck, steadied himself. "Is this really happening?" he asked, "Whatever *it* is?"

He had to wonder what was true. The night before had happened the way he had always wanted it to. He had always been the one who initiated sex throughout most of their relationship. It always seemed that in fact, on further thought, he had always been more concerned about giving her pleasure. She had never before given as much to him. When it came to pleasuring him, she had always gone about it in a mechanical manner. *In her mind, it must have been some sort of a wife's duty. It was like an afterthought for her when she got what she needed.*

But last night, it was almost as if he had been the director of his own film. It went down exactly the way *he* wanted it as though she actually wanted to fulfill his wishes. It was genuinely caring and not the fake acting like before. In fact, it was a really loving and erotic experience. *We were having long and meaningful discussions too, without arguing. Grace didn't seem so irritable and ready to pounce.*

Algernon leaped onto Karl Otto's lap. The cat had long ago resigned himself to approach him as a barely acceptable substitute whenever Grace wasn't there... and he wasn't hungry. Karl Otto sat back in his chair again and rubbed his eyes, trying to wipe away the idea that Grace was gone. "What does this mean? Am I dreaming that I was dreaming?" Pause. "Am I dreaming that she's dead or am I dreaming she's alive?"

He remembered a story he heard in college about the ancient Chinese poet, Basho. It went something like, "Was Basho dreaming he was a butterfly or was the butterfly dreaming he was Basho?" Reality was taking a double dip.

"Did my wishful thinking somehow cause our sexual experience and maybe Grace's death? Am I awake now and Grace is, in fact, dead? Or," he hoped, "is Grace alive? But if so, is she slated in some universe to die in an accident?" Pause. "Can fate be changed?"

Karl Otto tried to call Grace on her mobile phone. He pushed the auto dial like he had done thousands of times. There was a screeching noise followed by a voice that said, "I'm sorry. This number has been disconnected. Please check the number and try again." He did try again, with the same result. He tried dialing the number manually, but he received the same message.

Karl called the main number of the company where Grace worked. She worked for an advertising agency. The receptionist answered. "Hello, Kraplock, Kirschner, and Kramer." KKK. Karl Otto was too preoccupied to notice the ironic initials.

"Hi, this is Karl Otto. I'd like to speak to my wife, Grace Otto, please."

There was a very long pause… "You said this is her husband?"

"Yes, could I please speak to her?"

During the very long pause that followed, he could hear her staring at the phone while she held it away from her ear. "Hold on sir."

What seemed like an interminable three or four minutes passed before a man's voice answered. "Can I help you?"

"Yes. I'd like to speak to Grace Otto, please."

"And who did you say you were?"

"I'm her husband."

Long silence. "Sir, you are obviously not her husband. Ms. Otto died in a car crash months ago. I don't know who you are or what you're trying to pull here, but this is not funny. I'm going to hang up now." There was a click followed by dangerous silence.

He was doubting his own sanity. *What is this?*

Algernon tired of him and left for parts unknown. Cats always seemed so mysterious. *Maybe it's because their brains are the size of a walnut.* Sometimes Karl Otto wondered about Algernon's world. *Where does he vanish to? He appears and disappears like a ghost. We should have called him Phantom.*

Karl Otto sat thinking in circles most of the day. He was unable to do any of his work. He tried to watch the stream, but he just couldn't concentrate. Anxiety was getting the best of him. He'd start watching one program but soon disappear into unknown territory. His attention would return to the screen and he'd realize that another show was on the screen. *Where did the intervening time disappear to? Was it sucked down into Algernon's underworld? How much time has gone by? Where am I? I obviously wasn't watching the tube and I don't think I was asleep.*

He tried streaming a movie on his computer, but his attention waned so much that he couldn't follow the story. He felt sadness, confusion, and rage simultaneously. Should he grieve the loss of Grace? Should he search his memories to fill in the gap of those lost months? Was his anger and frustration justified? Then he said, "I'm too young to show the early signs of Alzheimer's disease. Or am I? Early onset?"

How could I forget a thing like that? The person closest to me with whom I just had sex last night has been dead for months in a tragic car crash, no less; and I can't remember it? Was I in the car too? Maybe I was and hit my head. Maybe I sustained a brain injury. Maybe I have amnesia for it. That might explain things... Maybe.

Karl went over to the kitchen counter where the ads and bills were still piled up. He hadn't gone through the whole stack again, yet. He threw out the ads and set the bills aside. At the bottom of the stack was a copy of the police report regarding Grace's accident. He stood there staring at it for a moment.

"Damn!" he said, "Step right up ladies and gentlemen! Nothing up my sleeve. Now you see it and now you don't." He unfolded it and read it for the first time in its entirety. It said that Grace was the lone occupant and that she had been hit broadside by a stolen vehicle driven by a man on a crack high in a police chase. It appeared that she probably died instantly. "At least she didn't suffer," he hoped aloud. His voice faltered with a sad sounding hoarseness. "So I wasn't in the car! So I didn't hit my head. Was I just so psychologically distraught that I wiped it from my memory?"

Karl Otto paced the floor as though he was going somewhere, but he just walked in circles around the house. He hadn't had this much physical activity in years. He realized he was drastically deconditioned physically. Maybe mentally? He tried to think of some useful activity, but there didn't seem to be anything to do. He exhausted himself pacing all day. "Maybe I should see a psychiatrist. No. All they do is dope you up with drugs. Maybe I should see a psychologist. Maybe I need someone to talk to. But then the psychologist might think I'm crazy and hospitalize me. What would I tell a therapist? I'm having sex with my deceased wife every night? Shit! I can't even open up to a professional stranger or I'll end up in the loony bin!" He was tired and when he looked at the clock on in the kitchen on the "food nucker" during one of his walkabout circuits through the house, it was six o'clock.

His pace was slacking to a crawl by now. He was physically and emotionally spent. He headed for the bedroom and stood there looking at the bed, their bed. He heard the sound of faint music as he landed. As soon as his head hit the pillow he was sucked down into the quicksand of Morpheus. It was like launching through the event horizon of the black hole of sleep. It swallowed him in a single gulp.

CHAPTER FOURTEEN
Jeremy Therapy Five:
John Doe Dreaming Memories

Their next therapy session was nearly a repeat of the previous one with the exception that John Doe was able to relax more readily and stayed with the memory longer. The process of recovering memories was moving slowly like a worm struggling to cross the path after a spring rain. Every session began with Jeremy's question, "did you make any progress in remembering anything more?" The answer was always the same, no memories.

John Doe said, "I did have some dreams, though." He was silent for a few minutes and Jeremy waited him out while the clock ticked on without hesitation, but there was the nanosecond gap of silence between tic and tock. John Doe said, "I did have a dream I thought I should tell you about. I don't think it's important, but I figured that you're the therapist and you might like to hear it." He hesitated. "I'm not sure if this is relevant Doc," he said. "It was very short. Just a flash."

He called the therapist 'Doc' even though Jeremy Lincoln had a master's degree in psychology and didn't have a doctorate. Jeremy Lincoln, to be fair, did try to correct him, once. Jeremy had gone on for his Ph.D. and completed all of his coursework, but he never completed his dissertation. He was what they called an A.B.D., "all but dissertation." He was secretly flattered by the misunderstanding and the status it carried. So, he had done his duty and informed John Doe of the correct situation... Once. Jeremy said, "It could be significant. Why don't you tell me about it?"

"Two nights ago, I had a dream. It was kind vague and fuzzy at first. I was in a car stopped at a traffic light and someone approached the window asking for my help. I remember rolling down the window. Then I woke up. That's all."

"You said, "at first". What did you mean? What was your reaction? How did you feel?"

"It became more vivid in the end." There was a deep pause while the gears meshed and his brain shifted from first gear to second and the images came into view as he rounded the mental corner on memory road. "I woke up in a sweat, it's probably nothing. It was probably just that I had too many covers on me that night or maybe it was the nasty sauerkraut I ate for dinner at the soup kitchen."

His therapist asked, "Do you think it might have something to do with the fact that you woke up laying in the street apparently left for dead?"

John Doe thought for a moment. "Hum. I hadn't thought of that. Maybe..." He appeared to be in deep thought. He was, in fact slipping into the depths of another world for the fraction of a sad second. "I'll have to think about that, Doc. I was in a car in the street during the dream."

"Okay," said Jeremy Lincoln, "I don't want to put words in your mouth or false ideas in your head." There was a thoughtful pause as he down-shifted into low gear. Jeremy broke the silence.

"Now I want to talk about your fears and anxieties. They may be preventing you from recovering your memories and your identity. I want you to consider adding something to your work here and at home, if that's alright with you. I think you're ready."

"That would be great, Doc. I'll try anything you think might help."

Jeremy had decided that John Doe was probably an educated man and that he was most likely used to being disciplined enough to write on a regular basis. "First, I'd like to get a better handle on how strongly you feel the fear and anxiety. On a scale of one to ten, one being no anxiety or fear, and ten being the worst and most intense fear possible. The level at which you can't stand it." Jeremy was trying to make the subjective emotional experience a more rational one. This, he reckoned, would cause John Doe's brain to dampen down the emotional brain and turn up the juice in the more rational prefrontal lobes.

"Well, Doc. I'd say when I was having that dream it felt like a nine or ten." He was doing a rational analysis of the feelings now.

"Okay, would it be fair to say that it's nine and a half?"

"Yeah. I think that's about right."

"Okay. So, when we do this relaxation and guided imagery here in the office we'll monitor your progress this way. Now, I think you're still doing this exercise at home. Am I correct?"

"Just about twice a day, every day, Doc."

"Okay. Since you have no computer or phone you can use for this, I have a pen and a notebook here." He handed it to John Doe. "I'd like you to take them and keep track of the level of discomfort you feel when you do it. Please note the date and time you do it and the level of discomfort you feel. As you can see, I've taken the liberty of drawing lines dividing the first page into columns. I have labeled them across the top. There's one column for time/date. There's a column for the level of discomfort and one for a description of what you remember. That is, what you experienced. In other words, the scene or story, what you were feeling, and the intensity you felt on the one to ten scale." Jeremy figured that this would not only keep a record of the progress but project the emotions onto the page and light up the prefrontal cortex. It would move the emotions into a more rational realm.

John Doe hid his skepticism about the benefit of trying to objectify his emotions. "Okay Doc, I'll try it."

"It's pretty subjective but it'll move you into a more objective mode and give us some measure of your progress. Most of it is jotting down numbers with the brief description of the scene."

"Alright," said John Doe.

"Okay, let's do this part, if it's alright with you. Please get into a relaxed state like you always do. When you feel you are at a level one, having no discomfort, raise a finger to signal me. I'll start you on the imagery. After we start on the imagery, if you get too uncomfortable, just stop and go back to the relaxation. Once you're relaxed, we can resume the image or, if you can't go on, if you are not able to get relaxed, just open your eyes and come out of it.

"Now," Jeremy continued, "close your eyes and relax. Signal me when you are relaxed and ready to proceed." The therapist sat and waited for the signal. The snail of five minutes inched by while Jeremy tried not to get too caught up in his own thoughts. But he couldn't help thinking about how difficult it must be for John to face his scary memories. The memories that had been too traumatic to rescue from drowning in the depths of his unconscious mind. Memories that were always lurking just below conscious awareness. He watched closely for the signal. Once he saw the first finger on the right hand flicker up, he paused for a second and waited for the dust to settle before he resumed his instructions.

"Alright, now we're going to slowly go back in time." he said in a soft, quiet voice. "You can reverse your steps. Let's start with the first time you came to the clinic. You can start by pushing the reverse button on your memory and, like a movie, follow it back through the scenes until you feel any discomfort. That's any discomfort at all. At that point, I want you to stop and relax. Signal me with your finger that you have stopped and you are calming down."

"Okay, Doc. Backward."

"So you're sitting in Ms. Harper's office and you get up and walk backward out to the waiting room then back out the door. Then you're outside and back to the bus that brought you from the shelter. Once you've started that backward journey, keep going until you feel uncomfortable. Stop and relax or come back here. That way you can go back and watch it like it's streaming on your screen at home. Signal me whenever you stop. If the time is running short I'll let you know and we can put a marker on that point in your memory. Call it a pause button or a bookmark. That way you can go back and pick up where you left off. Please keep in mind that, no matter how real they feel, these are only memories. You are not really there."

Jeremy Lincoln sat and watched closely for signs of distress. Jeremy was the only thread connecting John Doe to this world, but he began to feel the tug of that connection. He too was fading into John Doe's world. It was as if a vortex had raised its curtain and revealed its depths.

A cockroach checked into the roach hotel and a fly was trapped in the spider's web that had gone unnoticed. A mouse peeked out from a gap in the baseboards. All occurred outside of the therapist's awareness. The watch ticked by in Jeremy's ears and he could feel his heartbeat in his throat. But his eyes were intensely focused on John Doe.

Jeremy realized that he had to extract himself from the magnetic pull of the chasm. He grasped the arms of his desk chair, the only reality within reach, and reoriented himself. He refocused on John Doe's hands.

There were two points when John Doe signaled that he had stopped to relax. He had been seized with sensations of panic infused by the illusions of memory. Memories that he dared not share with his therapist. Sadness gripped him by the throat and he wanted to run from the paralysis of the recognized truth.

Jeremy saw the quickening of breath in John Doe's breast followed by a struggle to slow it and increase its depth. The time was getting short, anyway. Jeremy stirred and said in a gentle voice, "okay, we've gone as far as we need to go today. Please push the pause button and mark this spot in your memory. When you've done that slowly open your eyes and come back here to this time-space coordinate safely and comfortably." Jeremy was a sci-fi fan and thought of things in those pseudoscientific terms. He watched closely as his patient's breathing deepened and he gradually opened his eyes. He sat in a shroud of silence for a few minutes while he gathered up the scattered fragments of self.

At long last, he opened his mouth to speak, but no sound emerged until he cleared his throat.

"Haam!" He hacked up a tiny ball of anxiety into his throat and swallowed it back down. "That was interesting Doc. Thanks," he gargled.

The roach was dead, the spider finished its instinctual ritual, and the mouse disappeared under the bookcase. Still, no one noticed.

Jeremy asked, "Do you feel comfortable enough to tell me what you remembered?"

"Sure. I went back in time to the social worker's office and then on the bus to the shelter. It was a shadowy dream. I continued creeping through the memories until I got to the second time I passed out after running away from the scene of the crime. It seemed even scarier to fade out backward and reenter unconsciousness in reverse at the very point where I was supposed to be waking up. When I awoke in reverse, I had to stop and relax like you said to. After I emerged from the cave of fear and confusion, I was so foggy and disoriented that I stumbled backward. I continued back to the first time I passed out, not long after I began my flight. That was even worse than the second one. I was so dizzy."

There was a silence that permeated the clinic for a few seconds.

"I had to stop and relax again. It took longer to get through that ephemeral lapse of time, but I eventually did it. I don't think I could have gone any further back today. I was feeling disoriented, dizzy, and faint. Then you stopped me. I was about to stop anyway, but I almost forgot that I was here and not there. I was vaguely aware of being in two places at once. I had to struggle my way back. I was spelunking in a cave of memory a long distance underground and the only way I could get back to the surface was your voice, a rope of sorts, connecting me to the surface guiding me back."

"Wow. I never thought you'd get so far on your first try. Can you tell me what level of fear and anxiety you felt?"

"My experience of discomfort was about a six at the first break," John Doe determined, "but an eight or nine this last time which, was the first time I fainted. Geez! This is confusing." He frantically shook the cobwebs out of his brain while the spider on the corner of the wall paralyzed another helpless fly. The movement of his rapidly shaking head only caused his brain to slosh around in cerebral-spinal fluid inside his skull and make him dizzier.

Jeremy looked up the date and had him enter it along with his level of distress in the notebook. He made a brief note of the content of the memory too. They set that as a baseline for comparing future time periods spent in a memory and the intensity he felt.

Jeremy said, "You know, if you want, you can do the same notation with the dreams when you have them. That is, if you want to. You can record the same information, but just indicate that it's a dream instead of the guided imagery."

"That's a great idea Doc! Maybe I'll write the dreams in red ink."

"Sounds good to me." The red symbolism of blood was not lost on Jeremy. He was even more convinced that the dreams were probably the residual shards of memories like the many reflections in a shattered mirror.

The session ended and John Doe left the building with his notebook just in time to disappear into the bus that serendipitously pulled up at that exact moment.

Jeremy Lincoln was excited about the success they were having, but worried that it was progressing like a Cheetah rather than the Tortoise he had in mind. "But!" he said to the empty shadows in the corner, "he's eager and he's progressing."

The empty room felt reassured.

CHAPTER FIFTEEN
Curiouser George

George dropped John Doe off at the shelter and, as was his custom, he watched him through the side mirror. George stopped at the traffic light and continued to watch. Instead of entering the shelter as he normally did, John Doe kept walking in the opposite direction. *That was different. There were times that John didn't enter the shelter, but sat in the bus stop bench in front.*

About a block away, he waved at a car that pulled up beside him. George saw him slide into the passenger seat. The light changed and George put the bus in gear and pulled away while the car disappeared in the opposite direction. The green traffic signal screamed 'GO!' and the bus started up. The blue exhaust farted out the rear end and the roar of the motor bounced off the surrounding buildings and echoed through the streets.

Who picked him up? It seemed to be a woman, but I couldn't see her face. Could she have picked him up from the bus stop in the past too? Or maybe there were different people picking him up? This time he had been nearly a block away from the bus stop. George couldn't get it off of his mind. *Is John on drugs and his source is picking him up or is he the dealer? Maybe he's selling sexual favors to suburban housewives for cash. Maybe they pick him up there and return him afterward. Maybe it's an innocent thing.*

He struggled to keep it out of his mind, but it kept popping up. His brain seemed to suddenly bolt ahead leaving him behind, forcing him to catch up. He felt as though he was being dragged forward by his own thoughts. *Something funny is going on; I hope he doesn't get himself in a jam. What in deep hot hell is he up to?* He wanted to find out, but he didn't want to appear to be prying.

I'm worried about John. George was so caught up in his ruminations that he almost missed a stop and pulled over a little too abruptly. There was a collective gasp. The vehicle held its breath and a suffocating, but momentary, partial vacuum ensued. Realizing his mistake he yelled over his shoulder, "sorry folks, there was a car that nearly hit the bus and I had to swerve to avoid a crash," he lied. Two passengers looked frantically out the windows for the invisible errant car and one lady crossed herself. There was a collective sigh that filled the bus and the air rushed back in. Three people prayed.

George felt the cold perspiration rolling down is forehead. He felt shaky and tried to breathe deeply while three people boarded the bus and waited in line to pay the fare or use their bus passes. He tried to settle his jangled nerves while he waited for everyone to be seated before he started up. He breathed deeply and he felt his shoulders drop about a foot and a half.

CHAPTER SIXTEEN
The Case of Jeremy Lincoln

Jeremy Lincoln met with the treatment team that week. To him, it always seemed like an alien world filled with a mixture of good advice and cruel criticism. The psychiatrist, Dr. Suiminski, the social worker, Ms. Julie Harper, and two other therapists were also in attendance.

The room was hot and stuffy. When he gazed across the space it seemed as though he was peering through rising steam. Jeremy noticed a wavering in the air. Everything was undulating and swimming in the hot, damp atmosphere. But, simultaneously, the light seemed to dim more than it should have been with the shades sprung wide.

Dr. Suiminski shook Jeremy out of his reverie. "Jeremy, how's it going with your John Doe?"

Startled back to reality, Jeremy felt the sharp edge of piercing eyes stabbing him. He was sure that his approach to John Doe's treatment was tracking true, but he worried about the criticism of the others. In the past, he felt ambushed by the team's questions and oppressed by some of their "suggestions" that had the force of commands. Julie Harper was especially the most insightful and the most grizzly in her so-called "feedback". She was not loud or directly cutting, but the force of her opinions felt like an atomic bomb being dropped on a gnat.

Jeremy explained the approach he had been taking with John Doe. He explained that he was trying to help John Doe relax and then eventually, but slowly return to the last incident he remembered after he awoke. He said, "I thought if he could go there and remain increasingly relaxed, he might be comfortable enough to start recovering other memories. So far, he has reached the point when he passed out for the first time after the blow to his head."

Dr. Suiminski was frowning. Jeremy was acutely aware of this and he felt the fire igniting in his face, and it was spreading its burn all the way to his neck and down his chest. *Oh, oh!* The alarms went off and he began to stammer. "Sssoo..." Jeremy was accelerating more slowly now and the fire under the hot seat was stoking up causing his blood to boil. "I tried to do the best I could with him." Jeremy was sounding apologetic.

Doctor Suiminski said, "Aren't you pushing him too fast?" There was a runaway train bearing down on him. Jeremy was tied to the tracks facing the crushing force heading toward his self-esteem. "If you're going to take that approach, shouldn't you start with more neutral memories and slowly regress back to the upsetting ones? I'm worried that going too fast will cause him to seal off the scary ones even more because he's not ready for it."

Jeremy tried to cut the ropes and leap off the tracks before Julie Harper's diesel engine delivered the final blow.

"Well, I agree," Jeremy defended while trying to keep a professional tone and appear to be cooperative. He wanted to decrease the momentum of the massive train of criticism bearing down on him and make them think he was on the same page... at least in the same book. "I was trying to do just that." He tried not to sound too defensive. "I told him to go back to a comfortable place at first, even if it was only an hour or a day." He paused and cringed, and braced for the crash that didn't happen. He picked himself up mentally and started again. "But, during this last session, he went all the way back to the point where he passed out twice after being hit on the head. He did it on his own. He even reported a dream that I thought might be an actual memory fragment."

"Huh," said the Doc, distracting himself by examining his pen and turning it over and over in his hand like a baton.

Jeremy noticed that this behavior was consistent with times when the doctor was restraining his internal judgment and criticism while he searched for a more benign and less direct statement.

"That seems unusual for a PTSD patient... Seems too fast. Most of them take many, many months to even begin to face traumatic memories and years to resolve them. Not that it can't happen more quickly. But it is unusual."

Julie Harper, M.S.W. fanned the flames when she turned to Jeremy with a slight pseudo-empathic smile unaware that it seemed mean and threatening. That is, if you examined Chomsky's deep structure of language. Her sentences revealed her negative tone as did her facial expressions and her other body language most of which was hidden by the table due to her diminutive stature. But Jeremy simply felt the force of it. Analysis was unnecessary.

"I agree with Doctor Suiminski." She was leaning forward, as was her habit when addressing any peon unworthy of her ever-superior opinion. Jeremy had noticed that she always waited for Dr. Suiminski's opinion before she expressed her own, that always mysteriously sounded just like his, in different words. She seemed to be saying what the doctor really thought.

"Don't you think he's jumping into it a bit too quickly? On the other hand, if he's doing it so fast on his own, is this a ruse?" She had to add her skeptical 10X microscope's lenses, as usual. Sometimes, though, he realized, she zoomed in so tight that she saw the microscopic cells to the exclusion of the organism under discussion.

"Maybe," she said, "he's hiding out from the law or a crazed ex-wife or some criminals like he already said he fears. When you think of it, why would he think that someone is trying to kill him? There are many other possible explanations. Why did he pick that one? I just don't know…" She paused letting the right words carefully slither into consciousness and permeate the room. "It just seems unusual, that's all," she said with a definite blood red tint that colored her words and matched her hair.

A Napoleon complex? Maybe Josephine Bonaparte?

Jeremy felt as though he was really on the spot now and his defensiveness rose like the Hulk. He felt the heat of his face lighting up his awareness and he just knew everyone in the room could see him turn green. His body tensed and he felt his psychic muscles pop through his clothes. A roar was trapped in his throat trying to hold back, and simultaneously surging toward rage. He swallowed the glob and took his own advice. He breathed deeply and relaxed his muscles before he spoke. This was no easy task with all those eyes piercing his skin. "Maybe so," Jeremy finally said, "but John did it himself. Remember that he practices these exercises several times daily and that he is motivated to the point of obsession. We only meet every other week so he has lots of time to work on it between sessions. He has obviously dedicated his time and energy to it. It's all I can do to hold him back from jumping ahead. That's why I don't give him the next step until he has completed the one he's working on."

"Yeah," said Julie harper, "but he's going so quickly." Sarcasm was leaking out a bit more now in the surface structure of her words belied by her voice and the almost imperceptible negative shaking of her head. "It seems too smooth, too," she blurted out. She was instantly struck by her own tone and glanced around the room to see if anyone else noticed. No one dared move which made her falsely believe she had remained under the radar. Her ego visibly deflated which caused her to nearly disappear from view beneath the surface of the table.

Jeremy wondered why she never got a proper seat for her stature. He felt sorry for her. But then again, she could at least have found a cushion to prop herself up. *Maybe a phone book. Do they even publish those anymore?* Jeremy tried to regain his objectivity and drop his defensiveness. "Well, he does seem gung-ho about recovering his lost memories. It is his lost self, after all."

"Maybe," said Dr. Suminski.

Julie Harper still looked puzzled and skeptical, but nodded slightly as if to say, "maybe" in mock agreement with the good doctor... It is possible... I guess.

Jeremy realized that she was trying to regain her position as the psychic Siamese twin or at least, the sidekick, of the Doc. Jeremy said, "I'll try to encourage him to move more slowly."

They moved on and discussed cases of the other therapists, but Jeremy was barely listening. His heart wasn't in it. In fact, he could hear his heart beating in his ears. His bubble had burst. He thought he was doing something extremely helpful, but now... doubts plagued him. He stared out the second story meeting room window at the dirty streets and the cityscape that towered over the neighborhood buildings across the way. The sun was high in the blue, cloudless sky. The outside world was squintingly bright and devoid of shadows, stark and two-dimensional. He wondered if he was doing the right thing with John Doe.

It seems right, but maybe I'm too close to him and the process to see the pitfalls. He was pensive for a full five minutes. *I'll have to check my subjectivity at the door and wear my objectivity chapeau.* He smiled at the thought of a top hat full of cogitations. *I'll have to try and put the brakes on so he doesn't try to go too fast.* For a moment his engine had stalled. His thoughts were on pause.

Wait! John Doe is clipping along at his own natural rate. I'm not pushing him. He's pulling me along. If anything, I'm reminding him to be cautious. His thoughts and memories are driving him, but, he does pull over and rest whenever he's feeling too upset. Should I try put on the breaks? Should I just help him along at his pace while being at the ready to pull him back a little if he tries to go farther than he can go at a particular point?

A puzzled look infused his face. *But how I can be certain that it's the right time? Besides, my efforts to hold him back haven't been very successful so far. I don't want him to start struggling with me either. Would I be the cause of his delay if I protest too much?* He found himself alone in the conference room. Everyone else had exited, unbeknownst to him.

"I'll have to sleep on it I guess," he said aloud to no one. No one answered. The silence swarmed into the room and thickened into a syrup of doubt and confusion dripping from every crack. He paused and stared at the foreboding wall. "I feel exhausted and I have the rest of my patients/consumers to see today." He had two weeks to think it through, anyway. He tried to set it aside, but his doubts and personal struggle built up to the extent that it exploded into a sleepless night.

In part, he was fretting over John Doe, but there was the crushing weight of criticism he felt from Julie Harper and Dr. Suiminski. He tried to tell himself that they were only expressing their concerns, but they, and Julie Harper in particular, did seem to awaken the feelings he had as a child when his mother yelled criticisms at him. *Am I mixing up my professional work with my personal pride? Am I like Narcissus peering into the pool of John Doe reflecting myself to the exclusion of the welfare and opinions of others? Will Daffodils spring from my seat at the self-reflective pool when I die?* He lay in bed that night riding his runaway train of thought until he climbed into the sleeper car of his mind and drifted off into a fitful sorpor. He was exhausted all of the next day.

The Juxtaposition Paradox Charles R. Stern

CHAPTER SEVENTEEN
Peek-A-Boo

Later, when he was half asleep, Karl Otto's penis was, he gradually realized, getting firm and filling the hand that was holding it. A voice said, "Hey sleepyhead. What are you doing in bed so early? Did you miss me or is that a sausage you dropped from your breakfast in bed?"

Karl Otto was lying on his side, facing his side of the bed. He opened his eyes and saw Grace kneeling next to the bed. She had pulled back the covers, unzipped his pants, and was smiling at him. She leaned forward and kissed him. He stared at her for a moment before the dawn of full recognition arose. He scooped her into his arms. He held her tight. He forgot about his arousal for the moment... that is, just for a moment. "Oh my God! I'm so glad to see you!"

She said, "I'm glad to see you too baby." She hugged him back.

It seemed to Karl that they were behaving like they did back in the early days of their relationship, but more so. He pulled off his clothes and helped her slip out of hers. They dove deep into the bed simultaneously pulling the sheet over them in a tidal wave of passion. They made love for a long time. Two jellyfish slowly undulating at first, and gradually escalating into the fast and furious pace of two dauphin in a feeding frenzy. He wanted to please her and did all he could to do so. He was astounded that the more he pleasured her the more it aroused him. It gave him almost more pleasure than the previous night. It felt at least as exciting as when she had given him so much of herself. He did the same things to her that he had the other night and he added oral stimulation, as well. She returned the favor. It was clear to both of them that they enjoyed pleasuring and being pleasured by each other.

In the afterglow, they talked for a long time. They were more comfortably open with each other than he remembered them ever being. She fell asleep, but he was wide awake. After trying to sleep for an hour, he realized that by trying so intensely to force himself to sleep, it awakened him even more. *What a paradox, the harder I try to do the thing, the farther away it retreats from me.*

He quietly slid out of bed, his feet firmly planted themselves on the floor, and padded into the living room. He tried to watch the movie he had been streaming earlier, but was unsuccessful, again. His attention drifted to the point that the screen was watching him.

She awoke about an hour later and sought him out. "Karl. What's happening?"

"I couldn't sleep so I came in here. I didn't want to wake you."

She said, "What's wrong? How come you can't sleep lately, especially after we make love?"

"I don't know. I have a lot of work stuff on my mind," he lied again. He hated to lie to her, but he worried she might think he was nuts and, who knows, it could ruin this... whatever it is. *How indeed, do you tell the woman whom you love and, by the way, with whom you just had great sex and the most intimate conversation ever, that she is dead?* He stood and wobbled for a second while the remnants of sleep drained away.

She followed him to the kitchen. She yawned and stretched and shook off the tiredness. "I'm hungry. Let's order a pizza," she said.

"I'm starved too. I think I forgot to eat today."

They ordered a pizza delivery. When the doorbell rang, Grace was in the bathroom. She yelled, "Can you get it babe?"

"Sure," he said. He gave the delivery kid a tip and carried the box to the kitchen. Grace joined him. The cat smelled a potential meal and snuck into the kitchen. They took their plates to the living room to eat it while fending off the cat. They had long conversations about work and their feelings about recent news events of the day and they eventually got around to discussing their relationship. They agreed that their marriage was on the best footing it had ever been and they could see themselves growing closer too. They reiterated their love for each other and touched and kissed with a quiet passion.

Grace finally said, "It's getting late and I have an early morning. I've got to get some sleep."

"Me too," he agreed.

They stumbled off to bed. It felt like wading into a lake and stepping into a drop off and drowning in an ocean of slumber.

The Juxtaposition Paradox Charles R. Stern

CHAPTER EIGHTEEN
Jeremy Therapy Six:
John Doe Dreaming Deeply

When John Doe emerged into the office for his therapy session, Jeremy Lincoln greeted him with an offering of coffee. They sat silently trying to pretend to drink the pungent sludge for a few minutes before Jeremy breathed new air into the atmosphere. "So what has been happening with your relaxation and imagery exercises at home?"

"I'm still doing it. I get pretty relaxed and I think it helps me get to sleep."

"That's great John." He paused to reflect on the blast that still burned from the treatment team meeting. "Have you continued using the notebook?"

"Oh yeah, I have it here. It's the second one. I filled up the first one you gave me. Do you want to look at it?"

"Sure, if you don't mind." He handed it over to Jeremy.

The unexpected weight of the writing nearly caused the therapist to drop it. He had to redouble his grip. Its gravity seemed

---

to be tugging it Earthward. The therapist looked over the entries since their last visit. He looked up. "It says here that you had more dreams."

"Yeah, but none of them were the same as the other one. They were kind of scattered. You know, sort of fragmented and a little ephemeral. I don't know if they're significant, but I wrote as many of the fragments I could remember in case you wanted to see those, too."

"Thank you; I do."

"Yeah well, they're very different." John Doe used to believe that life was a rope that was tied to conception and passed through birth, past the milestones and signposts of life, and was eventually tied in a straight line to the final doorjamb of death. Now it seemed disjointed.

"What do you mean different?"

"Well, the longest one was about being chased by a mob of people."

"Oh yes, I see that one here on page twenty."

"I was running and running, but I came to a cliff. I looked down from the precipice at the thick fog and mist far below. I could only hear the river rushing over the rocks at the bottom. The mob was nearly upon me. I was surrounded and there was no way to escape around the mob. I'd either be caught and have to fight and probably be killed in the frenzy or jump off the cliff to certain death."

"I see. You were in a damned if you do and damned if you don't situation? "

"Yeah. That about says it."

"You say it's a different dream, but can you deduce a similar theme?"

"What do you mean, Doc?"

"It seems to be about a traumatic experience like your memories. You couldn't decide whether to go forward or turn back and it seemed dangerous either way." Jeremy interpreted. "You were overwhelmed by fear for your safety and there wasn't a good alternative. You felt you were damned if you stayed and damned if you fled. You could see no good alternative, no escape in both scenarios." *Maybe I'm being a bit too leading, but John is an intelligent and psychologically minded man. He is capable of considering an interpretation and accepting or rejecting it.*

"Yeah. Now that you put it that way, Doc. I guess you're right." He thought for a moment. "I guess the theme is similar, but it's not the same recurring one we've been talking about."

After a moment's reflection, Jeremy ventured, "Well, it may or may not be related. But they are all about traumatic experiences. It's also about having to make a decision with no good solution open to you. Have you been feeling like that while you are awake?"

"Maybe. I have been a little more uncomfortable lately."

Jeremy said, "Well just think about it. I don't want to put words in your mouth. Please correct me if I'm off base."

"Okay."

"Now, what else has been happening with you?" Jeremy asked. He wanted to distract from the topic for a moment to let the whole thing settle in unconsciously and to avoid any resistance he may have kicked up.

"Well, I might have an opportunity to get a subsidized apartment. At least, I'm on the list. Oh, and a janitor job may be working out, too."

"How do you feel about the possibility of an apartment?"

"I'll be glad to have the privacy, but I have the feeling that I'm capable of more. I just wish I knew what I used to do. I don't even know my level of education." His head sank slightly below the waterline of his consciousness as the ballast of frustration increased.

"That must be extremely frustrating," said Jeremy, empathically stating the obvious.

"Damn straight it is!" John Doe was starting to show more of his frustration and anxiety. The tightly knit fabric of his attitude was starting to show signs that it was fraying around the edges. Jeremy feared that he might unravel unless his optimism was recovered.

He needs more signs of progress, Jeremy said to himself. *The ship of his state of mind is beginning to leak. The sea of doubt is starting to wear at him.*

"Sometimes I feel as though I'm coming apart one plank at a time," said John Doe. "Why can't I remember!?" He was almost yelling. His fists were doubled up and his eyes rolled up and disappeared into his brow. His eyelids slammed shut in a tight squint screwing his face up into beet red and grotesque distortion of fear, frustration, and loss.

Jeremy saw the sinews and veins in his neck popping out as if the rivers of frustration were beginning to overflow their banks and carry him beyond the rapids toward the waterfalls of despair. Jeremy tried to help him calm down and slowly back away from the precipice. "You are feeling flooded with negative thoughts right now. You are feeling frustrated and the pressure is building up inside to the point that you think the dam is going to burst." Jeremy saw the whitecaps subside and begin to return to a more normal flow. There was a long silence while John Doe could at least tread water and breathe. Jeremy eventually threw in a floatation device and broke the silence. "So, let's stop and think for a minute. Are you up to it?"

"I guess so."

"Are you sure?"

"Yeah. I'm sure, Doc." But he realized he wasn't sure of anything lately.

"We need to continue navigating the waters we've embarked on, but let's back away from the dangerous monsoon for a moment."

"I know, but this problem is real Doc!"

"Sure it is. It absolutely is real. I meant no discount of its importance." John Doe's mouth was gold-fishing like he was out of water gulping for air. He was searching for something to say. Jeremy rescued him from his dilemma. "Glad to help. It's just that we have to deal with your emotions so we can reach your destination as smoothly as possible instead of jumping off the cliff."

"Okay. I understand. It's just hard when I'm so adrift every day. You have no idea, Doc."

"You're right. I can't imagine what you're going through right now, John. I imagine it's overwhelming." He hesitated long enough for the impact of the soothing empathy to soak in. "So how," Jeremy went on, "will these thoughts and feelings help you in reaching your goal?" Jeremy Lincoln wanted to distract his patient from the emotions into a more rational state to prevent him from being overwhelmed.

"My goal?"

"Yes. Didn't you say that you wanted to recover your memories and your identity?"

"Yes, I do."

"Okay. So how will these negative thoughts and feelings help you reach it?"

"I don't know." There was a long contemplative pause while the room looked on and listened intently. "I guess they won't."

"Okay. They may motivate you to some extent, but if they overwhelm you, drowning won't help. We have to swim at a vigorous pace, but avoid being sucked under by the greedy undertow of the reckless passion for success." For a few seconds, a shadow of silence fell over the office waiting for the next step before he began again. Jeremy thought, *we need to move toward resurrection without the wounds of lance and nail.*

"Okay John, take a long deep breath."

John Doe took several.

"Now take another deep breath in and hold it for the count of one thousand and five."

John Doe sucked in as much air as he could manage. His belly and chest swelled like a blowfish.

"Good, now let it out very slowly and relax your muscles at the same time. Come back to here and now. Let's escape from those overwhelming feelings for a moment."

John Doe slumped slightly in his chair. His shoulders sagged a little and his head drooped forward. Sisyphus with a moment to rest while his rock began its journey back down the hill.

"Okay. You were about to blow a gasket. I don't think you want that, do you?"

"No Doc. I guess not. It's hard, though."

"Of course it is. We knew from the start that it would be." Another pause. "Okay, take another slow breath in and hold it for the slow count of five followed by a very long exhale while you relax some more. Put yourself in the relaxed state you've been perfecting.

John Doe took a deep breath and closed his eyes in surprise for how quickly his shoulders slid down the mountain of anxiety in the avalanche of flaccid muscles. There was a pause while he let go and settled into a pool of floating flesh supported by his bones like a shirt on a coat hanger. He was becoming aware of his body mass and the weight of his trepidations pulling him toward more solid ground.

"Now remember," Jeremy reminded, "these are just thoughts. Your problem is real, but the thoughts are just thoughts. Your feelings are just feelings. They motivate you to some extent, but if they're too intense, they don't help you reach your goal. They aren't helping your immediate problems either. Even if they make you feel better for a moment or two, they do little to help you in the long run. Your memories are just that, memories. They aren't happening now nor will they ever be repeated. However, you're afraid of the emotional pain associated with them. We are trying to retrieve the memories with the least amount of distraction from the attached emotion."

"Is that even possible, Doc? It seems so real."

"Well, you can get to a point where you remember the incident, but, even if you feel some of the feelings, they will be temporary and less intense. Then you'll move on instead of getting stuck in your head."

"I see. I hope you're right, Doc." His skeptical tone was leaking off his tongue passed his teeth and lips and traveled out through the building and light years into the Milky Way.

"Try doing your relaxation exercise and step back from it for a minute."

"But Doc, I stay awake at night trying to run to the end of the never ending treadmill of memories that seem to be even more elusive the harder I try!"

"Okay. Maybe you're trying too hard. Sometimes the harder you try, the more difficult it gets because you get more tense and distracted by the effort. Let's start with the relaxation. Maybe that's why you're having those traumatic dreams. When you're asleep, you aren't trying and things pop up in a seemingly random manner." Jeremy was starting to realize that it might not be John Doe's unconscious resistance to recovering his memories as much as his conscious fears of what he'd uncover in the process.

They went through their routine again and, after a while, it seemed to Jeremy that the pressure cooker was starting to simmer down... a little... maybe.

Jeremy said, "Try to view the feelings and thoughts you're having as just thoughts and feelings. You're in a boat looking down into the ocean. You're not diving in. You're just observing. The things you see down there are like characters in a documentary movie. They're there, but they swim onto the screen and then they exit. Leave your attachment to them behind and look at them as though they were simply floating in and out of your awareness. Movies try to suck your emotions into the story, but you always have the option of pulling back and realizing that it's only a movie. If you fall in, you are a submarine coated with Teflon, nothing sticks to you. It's just like looking at a clock. You see the time, but you know it'll move on. You don't keep looking at the clock minute by minute and you don't keep thinking it's two o'clock all day."

Jeremy was aware of mixing his metaphors, but he was fishing for one that would catch on. "Your memories are of things in the past. They are no longer happening. You're safe here and now. You are a space alien peeking down into the happenings on Earth."

John Doe promised to keep practicing between sessions. To Jeremy, he seemed calmer, but inside, John Doe was weary. He was trying to extricate himself from his afflictions and of the poisonous fumes of memory. He left the session. Outwardly calm, but tormented from within.

"Just watch those thoughts and feelings," Jeremy reminded, "without taking them on. You're not a sponge. You are a submarine made of Teflon. A spectator. You can surface whenever you wish."

"Just a momentary lapse that's all," John Doe interrupted. "Okay, Doc. I'll keep practicing." John Doe visibly pulled together. "I'm alright now."

John Doe disappeared seemingly more relaxed. To the therapist, he seemed to be fading into the outside world that Jeremy could only imagine. This was an odd sensation that he had never felt about other patients. The frustration of the brass ring always had seemed to be just outside of his grasp, but now it might be in sight.

CHAPTER NINETEEN
Jeremy Therapy Seven:
Love at the Mall

John Doe had failed to attend his next appointment with his therapist. He called to say that he felt sick and had to cancel his session. He said, "I'll see you in two weeks at our next scheduled session. Sorry, I can't come today." His voice sounded distant as if he were using a bullhorn far away lost somewhere out there in a hazy mist on a ship at sea.

"Okay. Take care of yourself John. I hope you feel better soon," Jeremy said, a little too loud to compensate for the imagined distance. He sounded somewhat sympathetic seasoned with a dash of skepticism and a dollop of disappointment. It left a bad taste in his mouth.

"Thanks," said the faint voice. "I'll see you next time."

Two more weeks went by before John Doe drifted into the clinic for his next visit and docked himself in his usual moorings. The dead weight of his seat splashed down on the chair. He dumped into a sea of accumulated worries. Frenzied whirlpools of dust bunnies arose in such a cloud that, for a moment, John Doe couldn't see what Jeremy was saying.

Jeremy Lincoln noticed an imperceptible difference in John Doe. "Well John, are you feeling any better?" he probed.

"Better?" The cloud was lifting. Jeremy noticed the slight faltering in John Doe's voice. "Oh! Because I was sick two weeks ago? Yes I do, thanks."

"Where have you been?" Jeremy's voice arose in an expression that was so sufficiently understated that it was barely visible in the cloudy air.

Before he knew it, John Doe's head came up a little too abruptly revealing he harbored a secret. "What do you mean?" John Doe looked surprised. He felt so ambushed that he almost ducked. Blood on the wings of embarrassment flooded in and his face flushed red.

"I called the shelter to let you know I had an opening last week and that you could make up the missed session, but they said you were A.W.O.L. They hadn't seen you in several days."

"Oh. Well, I..." He stammered trying to buy time to think up a believable lie. He stalled for time. "I was kidnaped for ransom by Russian spies."

Jeremy said, "Very funny."

"The truth is, it was too late to get back to the shelter before they stopped taking people in. There's a curfew. I knew I'd be turned away so I found other places to stay for a couple of nights. Besides, I don't always stay there."

"For three or four nights? You must have been very busy to be too late for the shelter every night."

"Well, Doc..." A thought-filled gap slipped past them. It seemed to John Doe that an hour slogged by in a few seconds. Everything shifted into slow motion, thankfully defying the laws of nature and disproving Einstein's discovery that time is a constant. Sweat began to form on his brow and precisely one drop trickled down and stung his left eye. He squinted and wiped his eye. "To be honest with you Doc," John Doe finally admitted, "I met a girl. I spent a couple nights with her. That's why I was too late for the shelter curfew. She's homeless too. I met her at the shelter and we hit it off. She invited me to stay with her since I couldn't go to the shelter and I spent the night with her. A couple of nights. Well, more than a couple."

"If you are both homeless, where did you stay if you didn't sleep at the shelter?"

"As you know Doc, in the shelters you can't stay in the same area with the opposite sex if you're single."

"I see, but that doesn't answer the question completely, John."

John Doe was torn. He wasn't sure how to answer. "She stays at this shopping mall where she knows a way in after it closes. There's a spot where no one goes. Even the night shift security guards don't go there. There are no security cameras there either. It's a pretty nice setup."

"Why did she go to the shelter if she has such a nice place?"

"She goes to the shelter to take a shower and get cleaned up every few days. She also eats at soup kitchens and rescue missions at times."

Jeremy hesitated before his concerns tumbled out in the form of a question. "So did you sleep together?"

John Doe's face was instantly ablaze with embarrassment. "Sleep? Do you mean did we have sex?"

It was Jeremy's turn in the red zone. "I was trying to be polite, but yes, did you have sex?"

"Actually, we did, if you must know. It was pretty good too. I guess we were pretty horny, Doc."

"I'm just concerned whether you took precautions." Jeremy was trying to normalize the discussion by moving it into a reasonable therapeutic concern.

"Yes. She actually had some condoms. I hadn't thought to get any because I didn't anticipate having sex with anyone. She said that she had gone to the Planned Parenthood clinic for condoms and birth control pills. She said she had to be careful out on the streets by herself. She usually kept to herself, but we hit it off and either she grew to trust me or lust overrode her fears." He stopped for a second. "Well, she is pretty suspicious... well, paranoid. She said I seemed different than the others out there."

"Where is the shopping mall you went to?"

"I can't tell you."

"Why not?"

"I promised her I wouldn't tell anyone."

"Okay, but I was afraid that you'd get in trouble and end up in jail for trespassing or something. I really want to help you to remember your past. I can't do that if you are in jail."

"Okay. I'll be careful. I'm not sure whether we'll get together again or not anyway."

"Why do you think that?"

"She's afraid that someone will follow me and I'd lead them to her if I go there without her. She's very stealthy and makes sure no one follows her. The mall is quite a ways away too, so it's more difficult to follow her undetected. She's a little more paranoid now that I know where she lives. Apparently I'm the only one who does."

"Well, please be careful." John Doe was silent except for a very loud unconscious nod.

Jeremy was worried that John Doe was keeping things from him, but he rationalized this escapade as a private incident involving sex with a woman who swore him to secrecy. A one-time and understandable glitch in the therapeutic relationship.

There was a long transitional pause and Jeremy took the opportunity to change the subject while the dust settled into a thick carpet. "Have you had any more dreams?"

"No. Not since I last met with you… Oh! Well… technically, there were some, but I don't remember them, I just had the leftover feelings. I don't know whether any of them were the recurring ones. I don't think so. The feelings didn't seem the same. I couldn't write them down because there were only the residual emotions and they went out with the tide and remained engulfed by the ocean of sleep."

Jeremy thought he was beginning to see a little deeper into the fluid mind of John Doe. "I'm beginning to think even more lately, John, that they might not be simply dreams per se, but maybe at least some of them are fragments of memories."

A moment went by while this realization soaked through his skull and seeped into the gray matter, but it stopped just at the edge of consciousness. "Maybe, Doc. I don't know. I'll let you know when I remember another." They continued to practice the relaxation and simply recalling the imagery he already had.

John Doe drifted out of the office while the session followed him out the door and disappeared out into the sunlight.

Jeremy Lincoln usually remained in his office when his patients the Community Mental Health Department called "consumers," left. They called them consumers, he guessed, because they thought it sounded better than patient or client and after all, they were the source of the clinic's funding. They were consuming the services. Besides, they thought, there was a smaller stigma attached to it. But "consumer" sounded too commercial for his liking; as if they were picking out merchandise at the mall or like they were supposed to consume some kind of food. The word "patient" might make them feel like they were sick, and "client" might make them feel like they were in a legal situation like the lawyer's clients. Or maybe the client of some corporation trying to exploit them for their resources. However, it seemed ironic that the clinic still used the medical model of diagnosing and documenting cases.

This time, for a reason Jeremy was unaware of, he followed John Doe out into the waiting room and then to the outer door. He watched through the window in the door as John Doe boarded the bus. The doors closed behind him. Jeremy wondered what life was really like for the consumers he saw outside of their sessions. He heard their side of the story but didn't always get another perspective unless there were records from another agency or a hospital and police reports. Sometimes he heard stories from family members. But it was always from their prejudiced point of view. He especially wondered about John Doe. He was one of the most cooperative individuals he'd seen in his career and yet there was something about him that Jeremy couldn't put his finger on.

He peeked through the lobby door and watched the bus pull away and disappear down the street into John Doe's world. *Maybe it's a magic bus and his real name is Harry.* He smiled at this ridiculous analogy.

He returned to his office and mindlessly ate his brown bag lunch much too early while, immersed in wonder, he was awash with thoughts of John Doe. Like his consumer/patient, he was obsessed with the process of recovering memorable truths. He was unaware that his sandwich seemed to calm him as if it were a tranquilizer. *Maybe,* he thought absent-mindedly, *I'll go out for lunch later.*

The Juxtaposition Paradox Charles R. Stern

CHAPTER TWENTY
Over and Over

In the morning when Karl awoke, he turned over in bed looking for his sleeping wife. The cat fled, Grace wasn't there and there was no sign of her on the pillow. He got up and searched the house, but to no avail. He remembered that she had to be at work early. *Maybe she didn't want to awaken me and slipped out quietly.*

He went into the kitchen intending to make coffee, but he was distracted by the pizza box. He remembered that he ate three slices and Grace ate two last night. It had been a six piece pie. He stopped in his tracks when he saw three uneaten pieces and did the math. There should be only one piece left. He looked around for the coffee cup or a spent pod. *She never leaves for work without coffee.* There was no sign of cup or pod. He fed the cat mindlessly. Just a chore. No need to think about it. He had more important things on his mind.

He glanced at the pile of mail. Piles, that is. There was one pile of bills and the other stack was the insurance letter, the police report and the funeral note, along with the death certificate. There were no advertisements. He looked in the trash. They were still in there. *I knew I threw them away.* He stood there while the clock on the nuker ticked away for exactly a full minute, just staring at the mail. "Maybe Grace did it this morning before she left. But there's the death certificate! What's going on?!" He gave a fist clenching eye roll of intense frustration.

Slamming the papers down on the counter, he stood body rigid for what seemed like an entire season crawling by before he remembered the closet. He ran and opened her closet door.

"It's empty! Just the hangers!" His knees felt weak. He staggered back to the kitchen table and sat down so hard it actually hurt, but the pain in his head was an overriding distraction. His elbows found the table and his head dropped into his hands. He felt crazy. "What in the hell? What the fuck!"

Karl Otto's face was on fire. He knew what it meant. His blood pressure was soaring. He needed to calm down before something burst. *Am I dreaming such vivid dreams that I can't tell reality from fantasy? Am I hallucinating? Why, if Grace is dead, don't I remember her death? I must have arranged for her cremation and a funeral or a memorial service.*

"Fuck! Fuck! Fuck!" he heard his voice scream out in frustration. The explosion came from somewhere in the depths of his gut, a part of himself that he had never known existed, and blasted past his lips. It was uncharacteristic of him to use such language and he wasn't a violent man, but he felt like hitting something... someone, maybe. He had never before felt like his life was so completely and randomly out of his control. An oil slick of mystery and frustration had been set ablaze the waters of reason and his grasp on reality seemed to be dragged out to sea. He thought of the funerary rites of a battle-fallen Viking chieftain's boat set ablaze and sent adrift. Only he didn't feel that he was headed for the halls of Valhalla.

"I can't grieve my wife every day and have great conversations and sex with her every night!" There was a deep pause. "Can I?" His head was swimming. "I guess I am doing that now! Am I not?" He shook the waves of confusion out of his head.

He got dressed and went to the office. *What the hell. I might as well keep busy. Walking around the house and ruminating in ever expanding circles isn't doing me any good.*

Work was especially stressful. He had gotten nothing done the past couple of days so there was twice the work to catch up on today. It should have been a welcome distraction, but it turned out to be even more stressful because he couldn't stop thinking about Grace. *Better to ruminate here than at home. At least I can look like I'm working hard.*

If it was months since her death, assuming Grace really was dead, people would be finished with the condolences by now so they weren't as likely to approach the subject with him anymore. He remembered that it was Valentine's Day, so he skipped lunch and stopped at the card shop. He didn't feel hungry anyway. He bought Grace a nice card in case he really wasn't crazy. *If she shows up. If it turns out that I am really nuts, this would prove it. Wouldn't it? Probably. Maybe. Oh, crap! Maybe she'll return again tonight.*

He left the card on his desk where people passing by saw it. The rumor started circulating around the office that he had started dating again. The men said, "Good for him," but the women said, "It's a shame. It's so soon. He must not have loved her." He was oblivious to it all.

Karl was so far behind in his work that he had to stay very late to try and catch up. He could barely keep his head above water. His office door was open and the cleaning crew was already there acting, he thought, like he was in their way. They glanced at him periodically when they passed by his door.

At one point, Karl Otto felt a presence and looked up as a very round, black lady stood on the threshold of his office. She wasn't staring, really. It was more like a gaze. Her chin seemed to be lowered and her eyes seemed to be defocused with her lids at half-mast peering over her glasses. Her right foot was thrust out in front of her tapping slowly, rhythmically. It made her substantial body lean back oddly.

He felt an enormous discomfort and irritation welling up. He wasn't in the mood for this. *This is my office, she has no right to expect me to leave. I'll be happy to move out of the way for a bit, but this is ridiculous. All she had to do was to ask permission to disturb me for a couple of minutes!* Karl Otto looked up with irritation etched on his face. What?" he snapped, not really meaning to reveal his true feelings.

"Nothing," she said. She continued to stand there, but her face changed to an expression of, what seemed to him, a look of fear or revulsion mixed with... *What was it? Pity?*

He looked at her for a long time. There was something mesmerizing about her. "So?"

"Never mind," she said. She seemed to be squinting now the way one does when leaving a dark building and stepping into the bright sunlight. She was turning away, not due to embarrassment, but as if she couldn't look at him any longer.

He blurted out, "Hey! What's on your mind!?" He realized that he sounded angry. "Sorry," he said. He tried to soften his voice to a more friendly tone. "Please, just tell me what's on your mind. Do you need me to move out of your way so you can clean in here?"

She turned her face toward him, but she wasn't looking directly at him. She seemed to be looking somewhere about three feet above his head as though there was someone or something there. *A halo or the sign of the devil perhaps. What could she possibly see there? Maybe her eyes are beginning to roll back in her head and she's about to faint.* "Look. I'm not angry at you." He held his hands out with palms skyward to show that he had no hidden weapons in what seemed like a pleading gesture. "Just say what's on your mind. I promise I won't be mad at you." She was looking directly into his eyes now.

"You don't belong here!"

"What?" Now irritation was beginning to build into a tidal wave. "I've been working here for many years, thank you very much!"

"No... Here! You don't belong here, in this world. *This* world." She pointed toward the Earth. "Here!" she said with great force.

"What? Why? I don't understand you. What are you talking about?"

"You are an echo, a shadow here."

He thought, *this woman is crazy!*

She seemed to be reading his skeptical discomfort. "Sorry sir," she said. But she didn't sound apologetic. Her tone of voice sounded as if she felt pity for him! "I shouldn't say anything. It was a mistake. Forgive me." Her voice was anything but remorseful. She moved slowly away from the door with a slight limp. He could hear her pushing her cleaning cart down the hallway.

He yelled out, "thanks for the insight," in a half sarcastic tone. He shook his head in irritation. Didn't he have enough going on without *that*? He heard her enter the elevator and the office suite was deserted. Apparently, the rest of the crew had preceded her.

At about seven-thirty he thought he heard that music again, but it seemed like it might just be the vacuum the cleaning people were using next door. *No, they all left.* He was starting to nod sleepily. He dozed for about a minute when his phone rang. He looked at it and the display said it was Grace's phone calling him.

CHAPTER TWENTY-ONE
Amazing Grace

The telephone screamed for Karl Otto's attention. He answered on the fourth ring. "Hello? Karl Otto here," he said cautiously.

"Karl?"

"Yes."

"Where are you? I was worried because you weren't home when I got here and it's late."

"I had to work late. Sorry."

"Why didn't you call to tell me you had to work late?"

"I did try, but there was a message saying that your phone was out of order."

"You could have called my office."

"I know. I tried, but when I did, they told me you were dead. In fact they said you died months ago and hung up on me." There was a very long pause.

"What? Is this a joke?" There was an almost undetectable waver in her voice.

"Not on my part. They said you died months ago." Another pause.

"Who told you this nonsense?" She seemed openly shaken now.

"I don't know."

"What do you mean you don't know?"

"I didn't ask his name."

"Well, I'm going to get to the bottom of this tomorrow. That's not a funny joke!" She was silent for a moment. "Maybe you had the wrong number and there was another Grace they were talking about. The phones have been acting up lately. Maybe sunspots or something."

Sunspots? Well, I guess that's as good an explanation as any other. "Maybe," he said reluctantly.

"When are you coming home?"

"I'm wrapping up now. I'll be home in thirty or forty-five minutes, depending on traffic."

"Okay. I'll rustle something up for us to eat."

They hung up. He shut down his computer and headed for the elevator. There was a ding and the doors wrenched open. He stepped in. The doors lurched closed. Karl Otto felt a strange sensation that he took for fear. Fear, he assumed, for the seemingly old rickety elevator. *If this elevator gets stuck, I'll die before they find me or if I'm alive when they find out where I am, I'll be dead before they get this ancient sarcophagus open.* But then, this building is not that old. *It was built only about eighteen years ago. The elevator shouldn't be in this state of disrepair, at least, not to this extent.*

It was as though he had stepped into another world and the door cut him off from his. After hesitating for a few seconds, he shook off the sensation and pushed the button for the lobby. His worries about the elevator vanished behind him, along with the elevator, as he stepped out into the lobby. He headed for the parking garage across the street. He walked up to the third level where he had parked his car. Somehow, he just didn't want to face another elevator. He unlocked the car and got in. Another wave of sensations washed through him. He shook it off and started the car. He pulled out of his space, pointed the car down the ramp, and headed home. He called Grace to tell her he was on the road, but there was no answer. He tried again, but there was that message again about the phone being no longer in service.

She just called me on it! Something's wrong with the phone again.

He arrived home possessing no memory of the ride. He closed the garage door behind him and another odd sensation rustled through him like dry autumn leaves in the wind as though something was being blown out of him or passed him, perhaps. *Weird,* he thought, as he entered the house.

He took off his coat and hung it up. "Is that you Karl?" It was Grace's voice.

"Yes, it's me." He hesitated before blurting out his question. "You didn't answer when I called you to let you know I was on the way. Did you go out and forget your phone?"

"No. I was here the whole time. It was in my purse in the bedroom and I didn't hear it. Sorry, I didn't mean to worry you."

He shook his head like a dog shakes off the water after a swim in the ocean. *I must be going crazy.* "Well, when I called, there was a message that it was out of service."

He found Grace in the bedroom. She was fixing her hair in the bathroom mirror. The cat was perched on the counter and turned his head and looked at Karl Otto as if he were an intruder in his own house. "Did you bring food in or should we order out?"

"No, I thought we'd try some frozen things in the fridge we can cook. I took some out to thaw."

"Okay. I'm starved. Busy day at work. No time for lunch."

He took off his work clothes and got into jogging pants and a T-shirt and turned on the stream in the living room. The Valentine's Day ads were in full force. He remembered the card. He went back into the bedroom and retrieved it from his jacket pocket and quickly signed it. He wandered into the bathroom and hugged Grace's half-naked self. The cat jumped down from the counter and ambled off communicating that he wasn't leaving due to the intrusion, but because he merely felt like it.

He said, "Happy Valentine's Day baby!" He handed her the card. She took it automatically and stared at it for exactly five heartbeats. She opened it and read the inscription. She looked up at him.

"Thank you, Karl. It's very sweet." She paused with a pained expression. "I didn't realize it was Valentine's Day. I feel bad. I didn't think to get you a card."

"That's okay, babe. Your love is the only Valentine I need. That's enough for me." He grabbed her and crushed her against his body, picked her up, and spun her around.

She giggled like a schoolgirl, "Put me down, you oaf!" Once she lighted on her feet, she kissed him deeply. He let go of her and they stood looking at each other hungry for food and sex.

As though they were of a single mind, they decided on food and then sex. They remembered the time it was the other way around and they felt like they were starving afterward. Grace busied herself in the kitchen.

The Juxtaposition Paradox   Charles R. Stern

CHAPTER TWENTY-TWO
Jeremy Therapy Eight:
Pieces of Dreams

The next two therapy sessions with Jeremy were partly devoted to John Doe's fears that he might never remember who he was or what his previous life was like. Of course, they continued to drift through their relaxation and imagery exercises trying to float down the river of memories while avoiding the rocks and white water rapids whenever possible.

Jeremy said, "Your fears seem to be connected to your negative thoughts. Sometimes you're a fortune teller predicting the future and catastrophize about your chances of finding the end of your journey. These things are understandable, but they also distract you from steady progress."

John Doe shrugged and looked away. "That's for sure, Doc." John Doe was sitting in the office across from the therapist for the... *how many sessions had there been?* He couldn't remember.

"Well John," Jeremy Lincoln said, "what progress are we making toward recovering your memories?"

"No memories… but." There was a long hesitation.

"But?" Jeremy prompted, tinged with a tad of impatience reflected in his voice.

"Well, I had that dream again that I told you about a few weeks ago."

"The one where you rolled down the car window when a stranger approached?"

"Yeah, but it was a little longer this time."

Jeremy sat up straight in his chair and leaned forward. He penetrated the mental force field that always seemed to separate them with obvious interest and rapt attention. "Why don't you tell me what happened?"

There was a long pause. "The guy came up to my car and I opened the window like before because he seemed distressed and I thought he might need my help. But this time, he pulled a gun from his pocket and pointed it right at me!

"Wow. That must have been terrifying! What did you do?"

"I thought I'd push the button to roll the window up. As if that would protect me if he decided to shoot." John Doe offered a halfhearted, but anxious and truncated laugh. He was starting to become absorbed in the misty shadows of the past obviated by time and the mental distortions of recall.

Jeremy noticed a sadness spread between them. He recognized that he was feeling the tugging power of John Doe's experience too. He had to pull back from the vortex. "What were you feeling John?" he asked, sounding a little desperate.

"Terrified!" John Doe responded as though that was a stupid question. He was rubbing his neck and shaking his head. He looked like he was a bell ringing out a conscious alarm. "It seemed so real!"

His eyes were closed and, it seemed to Jeremy, they fluttered imperceptibly. "What number of discomfort, from one to ten, did you feel?"

"I'd say it was an eleven, Doc!"

"It was more than the scariest thing you could ever imagine?"

"Oh yeah... Well, as far back as I can remember, anyway."

"Was there more?"

"No. I woke up in a swamp of cold sweat. My sheets were soaked and I felt as though I was a creature dragging myself out of a bog. I was a little disoriented at first. You know, how you feel sometimes when you first wake up."

"Do you still think that your sweating was due to hot blankets or something?"

"No. When I woke up all my blankets were far flung. I must have kicked them off."

"Wow. Did that disturb the others in the shelter?"

"No, I don't think anyone was awake enough to notice."

"What do you think about the gun and all? Do you think it might be a memory?"

John Doe made a gesture of resignation. His shoulders hunched and he opened his palms toward the sky in an expression that seemed so say "of course, what else could it be?" He was starting to surrender to the fact that these were really memories invading his slumber. "It sure was frightening. It seemed so real,

Doc!"

"Have you ever had that experience in real life?"

His eyebrows arched and his head shot up, and he looked at Jeremy. "What? A gun pointed at me? No! Maybe. Not that I can remember," he said in a feeble attempt at a joke. John Doe was unconsciously, but unsuccessfully, using humor to deflect the conversation away from his feelings.

Jeremy recognized the distraction and changed the subject before a whirlpool of emotion swept his patient away. He wanted him to calm down so he could let go of the tension and anxiety that was riding on the storm front of memory. "Let's do some relaxation work for the rest of our session. We'll let the winds subside for now. You've done a lot already today."

"Okay, Doc."

"Did you continue the exercises between sessions?"

"Yeah. I had to go to the library down the street from the shelter to find a quiet place. They have a private reading room with comfortable chairs that you have to reserve. Sometimes I did it in bed at night when I couldn't sleep and no one else was awake. There was less noise and distraction."

"Did you keep writing in your notebook?"

"Yes. He picked up the plastic shopping bag he used for a valise. "I purchased this one for a dollar from the Dollar Store. I filled the others. This is the third one." He played go fish in his plastic valise for a bit longer. "Here it is."

He handed it to Jeremy. It had several pages heavily laden with John Doe's comments and ratings. Jeremy looked up. "Great job!" He was obviously gratified to have such a motivated patient. Jeremy thought, *it's rare to find such a cooperative pa... I mean* consumer, who made such rapid progress. It's probably because he's an intelligent man and he is not mentally ill. He can focus on a goal and stick to it. Besides, he's highly motivated... But he's like a freight train barreling toward the station. I hope the tracks ahead are intact and he doesn't end up on a siding or derailed in the attempt. Jeremy asked, "do you find the exercises and writing in your journal helpful?"

"I think so. At least I'm getting more relaxed and the memory of lying in the road isn't as scary. When I look back at the journal entries in the books, I realize how much progress I'm making. I wish I could come here every week so we could make even more advances."

"I wish we could too, but the budgeted money only allows for every other week and I had to fight for that because the funding agency only wanted to approve once a month."

"Oh. I see. Well, it's working, Doc. That's the important thing. I'll just try to step up my practice."

"How do you feel about doing another exercise right now, John?"

"Fine," he lied. He didn't really feel like doing it, but he didn't want to seem resistant.

"Alright. Take a deep breath." They went through the process that John Doe already knew, but Jeremy wanted him to practice it again before he left.

When they were wrapping it up for the day, Jeremy spoke. "I'm glad you continue the relaxation and imagery at home. It might be good for you to jot down any thoughts and comments that come to mind as well. But don't push yourself. Take it one step at a time. Don't try to skip steps. We need to prevent setbacks."

"Sure Doc. I can do that. I'll do anything that might help." John Doe suddenly brightened. The spotlight of consciousness came up on stage and isolated him in the room. "Oh! I almost forgot. It looks like I may have gotten the job as a janitor at a church three days a week."

"That's great, John. I know Ms. Harper, the social worker you met the first time you came, is also looking for housing and maybe a room and board, so soon you won't have to stay in shelters. You'll have more privacy."

"Thanks, Doc. You guys have been very helpful. I appreciate all you're doing for me." John Doe left the office and walked out of the building. He disappeared into the waiting bus. The door closed leaving Therapy World behind.

CHAPTER TWENTY-THREE
Curious Karl

Karl Otto hesitated for a second, but overcame his ethical quandary and walked over to Grace's purse on the dresser and fished for her phone. He opened it to her recent incoming call list. His call wasn't listed there. He took out his phone and called her number. He heard a ring tone through his phone as though the call was going through, but her phone didn't ring. Then that voice came on the line stating that it was a disconnected number. He shut off his phone. He sat her phone on the dresser.

He remembered that he needed change for his lunch and searched his junk drawer. His hand settled on something and he fished it out. It was Grace's phone! *Very strange, maybe I threw it in the drawer after she died?* "Honey, did you change your phone number or block mine accidently?" He yelled from the bedroom. He dropped the phones back in their respective places.

"No. I don't think so. Why?" she yelled back from the kitchen.

"I was just wondering why you didn't get my calls. Just check it okay?"

"Okay."

"Anything I can do to help in there?" he asked. *Please?* He was worried that he'd have to swallow it no matter how it tasted... whatever she was cooking.

"No. It's all fine," she yelled back.

It still felt strange that Grace was cooking and even stranger, that she was happy about it. She genuinely seemed to want to please him. He was determined to eat whatever she cooked without complaint, no matter what. After all, it was edible food. Probably. *Weird.*

They ate mostly in silence. The food wasn't bad. At least it really was edible. They passed some of the time mired in a few pleasantries and mundane small talk about work and household budgets. Avoiding the thousand-pound gorilla in the room. They rinsed the dishes together and put them in the dishwasher and settled into the living room to watch the news.

Algernon was curled up on Grace's lap lying on his back, enjoying a belly rubbing. She said, "Oh! By the way, I asked around at work. No one talked to you yesterday. Maybe it was a wrong number."

"Well, I pushed the auto-dial for your number. It always worked before. The same for your work number."

"Maybe there was something wrong with your phone again."

But he knew he called the right numbers yesterday.

"I didn't tell them what you said about someone telling you that I died. So I don't know if you called the wrong number, or what."

"Okay. Maybe. Sorry." He thought for a minute. "Maybe I'm losing it in my old age," he said, half-joking.

"Not possible," she joked, "you can't lose something you never had!"

"Ha, ha, ha!" he said with a sarcastic yawn. It felt good to be bantering instead of fighting.

She yawned and followed suit. He quietly shut off the stream and, looking like Zombies on the march, they slouched, shuffled, and lurched toward the bedroom. He undressed and crawled under the covers. Grace spent time in the bathroom doing exactly what, he had no idea. She always said she was getting ready for bed. Whatever that meant. It seemed to him as though she didn't look much different coming out than she did going in.

She doesn't really need makeup to be attractive. To him, she was always beautiful. Of course, she never believed him when he told her so, but she was secretly flattered even if she thought he was delusional, or lying. In fact, she would look away and, with a Mona Lisa smile, she would say, "Liar!"

She finally came out of the bathroom naked and slipped under the covers. He held her close. She snuggled into his arm. They talked about their relationship and how it seemed to be much better lately. It was getting more intimate than ever and they were having more honest and open conversations now. A second wind seemed to blow into the room. They felt the rising energy of intimacy welling up.

Eventually, she reached for his penis. He was already standing at rigid attention. He reached down and stroked her thighs for a while and eventually moved up between her legs. A few minutes later he entered her. She swooned. He held himself back as long as possible before he let go. Karl Otto wanted to give her the most pleasure he could. He wanted this new level in their honest and open closeness to continue and he was going to do everything he could to make it so.

He rolled off of her and pulled her close. Her body quaked as though she had another small orgasm. She seemed satisfied. They held each other for a while. Just as they were falling asleep, they migrated to their own separate sides of the bed. Except, she noticed that he had been sleeping on the opposite side than he usually claimed for his territory. *Oh well, maybe he wants to try something different in our relationship. Anyway, I like it better this way. It's more comfortable for me somehow.* She drifted off.

Upon awakening, Karl Otto anticipated that Grace would not be there just as before, but she was in the bathroom getting ready for work. She came out of her secret bathroom layer. She stood and hesitated long enough to view the man lying there. She half walked, half strutted over and knelt with one leg on the bed. She bent down to kiss him. "I've got to go babe. Have a good day."

"You too." When she walked out of the bedroom, he leaped out of bed and slipped into his jogging suit.

The cat fled to his basement underworld. He heard the garage door open. He ran to the door connecting the garage to the house and peeked out of the window in the door. There she was. The garage door was open and she was starting the car. He ran to the front window to watch her pull away. He waited, looking out the window. He heard the garage door close, but despite waiting for five minutes he didn't see her leave. He ran back to the connecting door and looked out. Her car was no longer there and the garage door was closed. *Something is wrong here.* He picked up his phone and dialed her. The message was the same as before. Disconnected.

He dressed and went to work. No sense in being late, especially with the backlog of work he still had piling up in his email inbox and voicemail, not to mention all the social media that was no longer just social, but commercial fodder for advertisements and other junk mail.

He emerged into the office only three minutes late. He told the receptionist there was a traffic back up on the freeway. He sat down at his desk and booted the computer. He searched for his wife's name. Thirty-five hits were easily filtered out using her birthdate and address. Her name came up. He scrolled to the last lines and found that it said she had died in a car crash! He just sat there stunned. "Unbelievable!" he muttered under his breath. "This has to be a mistake!"

John Jeffords, a coworker from the next office, was passing by and heard his exclamation and stepped in. "How are you doing Karl? Are you alright? You don't look so good."

Karl Otto looked up startled. "Thanks a lot! Just what I needed today, John." There was an awkward pause. "Look at this John. What do you think about this?"

John saw the name on the screen and read the obituary. "Well, it seems like a nice obit, Karl. It's a beautiful tribute to your wife now that she's... You know."

"Dead you mean?"

"Well, yeah. It seems nice. The obit I mean, not that she's..." John Jeffords opened and closed his mouth gold fish-like, but stopped himself in awkward silence. Then, "see ya later Karl." His voice trailed off and he drifted away back to his office. A ghost fading away into the gloom.

"Okay. Thanks." Karl Otto said, not noticing John had already disappeared.

Karl Otto decided to tell his boss that he was going to take the day off. He said, "I have some issues that came up unexpectedly regarding Grace's estate I still have to clear up." His boss reluctantly approved it.

He left the office and headed to Grace's old office. When he walked in, all eyes were plastered on him. Heads turned when he walked by. He tried to ignore it and strode up to the receptionist. "I'm Karl Otto, Grace Otto's husband."

"Yes, Mr. Otto. We've met a couple of times at company functions. I'm sorry for your loss. We all miss her around here. What can I do for you?"

"Well, I was wondering if there were any papers of a personal nature that Grace may have left behind."

"Not that I know of, but I'll call Mr. Bigelow, my boss. Maybe he can help you."

She called her boss. He emerged from his office and strode across the reception area with his hand outstretched. Karl Otto's hand thrust out suspended in catalepsy. Mr. Bigelow grabbed Karl Otto's hand in both of his and shook it vigorously. "Sorry for your loss, Mr. Otto. Grace was a great person and an excellent worker. We all miss her." There was an awkward pause. Mr. Bigelow said, "Now, what can I do for you?"

"I was wondering if Grace might have left behind some papers of a personal nature. I'm trying to tie up loose ends, you know, and I'm searching for anything that might help."

"No. I don't think there was anything left after we shipped her things to you."

"Okay, I was just wondering. It was a long shot. I happened to be driving by and I thought I'd stop in and ask." He made a one-quarter turn as if to leave and stopped. He turned back toward Mr. Bigelow. "Oh, by the way. Have you received any strange calls lately for Grace?"

"Well, now that you mention it, some guy did call the other day asking for her claiming he was her husband. I hung up on him." Then in a feeble attempt at humor, "you're the only husband she had right?!" He tried to laugh, but no one else did, so he stifled it. Another awkward moment slogged by.

"Well, thanks anyway." He shook Mr. Bigelow's hand again, turned and walked to the elevator. The door closed separating him from Grace's old world.

On the way out of the building, he was deep in thought. *What am I really trying to do here? Grace appears to be dead. Mostly. The only place she seems to be alive is in our house! The only time she's alive is at night. That's where we used to spend our time together unless we went out for dinner or spent an evening out with some friends. We went to a performance or a concert once in a while or a movie, but those nights totaled about ten or twelve times a year. If she's dead, there won't be invitations from her friends to get together anymore. Probably. Maybe it isn't so bad after all. But will she keep coming home to me every night or will she eventually fade away?*

"Well, he answered himself aloud, "even if I am hallucinating, at least I seem to have her for a while. That's longer than I would have had her now that she's dead. I guess. But what about the kids? They believe she's dead. What will happen if they come home for visits? I'll have to figure that out later. I'll have to find the answer this puzzle first."

But, Karl Otto wondered, *should I try to find out? If I uncover the truth, will it ruin everything? Will it all dissolve? Will I finally lose her forever?* He shook his head in total confusion. He realized that he was ruminating again about things he had no control over. He wasn't used to feeling helpless. Well, not totally helpless, anyway.

He felt very tired. He sat in his car for a while thinking. His eyes were getting drowsy and there was that damned music again. He reckoned that he must have dozed off for a second because he was startled awake when the phone rang. It was Grace. "Working late again babe?"

"Yeah," he lied. "I tried to call you, but I don't seem to be able to get through to your phone anymore. Maybe I need to upgrade my phone. Anyway, I'm just getting ready to leave now. I'll be home in a half-hour, unless you want me to pick something up."

"Oh yeah. Do you mind picking dinner up? I'm too exhausted and it's too late to cook."

"Okay, I'll pick up Chinese." He asked her what she wanted, but he already knew what she usually ordered.

"Egg Fu Young."

"What?" He didn't remember her ever ordering that.

"Egg Fu Young," she repeated, a little louder, as if she hadn't spoken loud enough for him to hear her. After all, there seemed to be something wrong with the phone.

She probably thought I couldn't hear her because my phone is dying. "Egg Fu Young? Since when do you like that?"

"Silly, I always order that."

"Okaaay." *Can things get any weirder?* "See you when I get there," he said.

He hung up the phone and called the Chinese restaurant, and ordered. A disembodied female Chinese accent said, "It will be ready in fifteen to twenty minutes." *Perfect.*

When he arrived at home, Grace's car was in the garage and the garage light lit up. He pulled in and pushed the button to close the door. He got out and went into the kitchen, "I'm home with Chinese," he yelled.

"With Chinese? What's his name?"

"Fu."

"Fu?"

"Yeah, Fu Young!"

"Oh, Mr. Young! He sounds yummy! Do I get him all to myself or is this a menage?"

"No. You can have him. I'm going to get into Cookie."

"Cookie?"

"Yes, Cookie Fortune."

"She sounds delicious. Maybe we could have a foursome!" She giggled and he was happy to banter and joke with her. It was refreshing. "I'll be out in a minute!" she yelled back from the bathroom in the master bedroom.

What's happening? Grace has a sense of humor all of a sudden after all these years? She used to have one, but it was very narrow. There were only a few things she found funny.

Grace donned a robe to cover and warm her nakedness, and padded into the kitchen in her bare feet. By the time she got there he had dished out the food into plates and bowls. He had placed the fortune cookies on each of their plates. They sat in the living room and watched the news on the stream while they ate.

They broke open their fortune cookies. His said, "Look to the future. Abandon the past."

Her fortune said, "Look for clues to the future in the present."

When they finished eating, he took the dishes into the kitchen and scraped and rinsed them, and put them in the dishwasher. When he went back to the living room. Grace wasn't there. He felt a shiver of fear traveling down his spine. He turned off the stream and hollered, "Grace?"

His relieved ears heard her voice coming from the bedroom. "I'm in here getting ready for bed."

He sighed with great relief. He could picture the two of them in there. Algernon on his perch watching her do whatever mysterious things she does. Probably taking off what she had put on in the morning that only made her look a little different than without it. "Okay, I'll be there in a minute."

By the time he finished tidying up and entered the bedroom, Grace was already under the covers. He stood there for a minute just staring at her.

"What's going on?" she asked.

"Nothing. I just wanted to look at you. I'm just so happy to see you. I just love you, that's all."

"Oh yeah?"

"Yeah."

"Well then, come here, lover boy." She stretched out her arms and wiggled her fingers inviting him in. "Show me!"

Karl stripped off his clothes as quickly as he could. He damn near tipped while dancing on one foot trying to get his right leg free of his pants in his hurried scramble to get to the bed. He dove, or should it be said, he fell into bed and jammed himself under the covers.

Grace giggled, "Graceful! Thanks for the show."

"Glad to entertain your fancy," he grinned.

She snuggled up to him. "Well, I hope to tickle your fancy." She paused while a more serious expression spread over her. She said, in a soft sexy voice, "I've been thinking about you all day. I've been thinking about giving you pleasure. And I've been wanting you to fill me up in every way with your love." She gently palmed his penis.

By this time, the cat was disgusted and left with a haughty flick and meow. No one noticed.

Karl Otto was so aroused that he finished much sooner than he wanted to. He wanted it to last longer. Karl reached for her and pulled her close. He kissed her and searched for her body under the covers. He pleasured her until she had two more orgasms. Then he went under the sheets and rendered oral stimulation. Another spasm shot through her. He climbed up into her arms. He was aroused again and lasted a lot longer this time. He hadn't recovered his virility so quickly since he was a young adult. Exhausted, they kissed and soon fell asleep.

In the morning, Grace was gone. No sign that she had been there. Algernon was asleep on her pillow.

No matter. We're having a better relationship than we ever had when she was alive... He paused. "What the hell. I am having intimate conversations, sharing great meals, and having the best sex we've ever had with a dead woman! I'm turning into a necrophiliac and she's turning into a nymphomaniac. Hum...they both start with N. "But she didn't feel dead. She felt more alive than ever. Can hallucinations feel that real? We talk intimately, we haven't had the tense arguments we used to, and we're having better sex than ever." He repeated aloud to Algernon who seemed to be saying, "You're repeating yourself... Boring!" The cat was nonplussed and simply stared at him as though he was the lunatic he felt he might actually be.

Karl Otto couldn't get any of it off his mind all day. He had stayed home again, but he had trouble concentrating on work. *This has been good. In fact, it's great! Why rock the boat?* He decided to accept the fact that she was dead and that she came back to be with him every night... *Weird. Is it morbid? Am I crazy?* "I don't care if it's a hallucination or whatever it is. It's great and it isn't interfering with anything or anyone else. What's the harm?" he argued with himself. He paused and thought. He was torn between the wonderful situation at night with Grace and the daytime reality that she was dead and his impulse to puzzle the whole thing out. *What's wrong with it?* He couldn't think of a thing....*Well, only that I must be lover to the living dead. But no one knows about that. So what's the harm? But, it's weird, it's psychotic. Maybe. Oh, crap! I don't know!* He gritted his teeth, bent his head toward the heavens, and lifted his doubled-up fists above his head and screamed. *Ahhhhhhh!"*

This sent the cat flying away and back into his phantom world. It was as if he was cursing God or the fates or something. But it nagged him that he had no idea why this was happening.

"She's not a ghost. At least not like the books and movies depict them. She is solid, substantial. Not ephemeral at all! She is as real as I am. No doubt about it. It's as if *she* died and *I* went to heaven!" He paused. "Or is this heaven by night and hell by day?" Then he stopped for a moment.

Whatever this is, I'm getting everything I want. Grace is more loving than I've ever known her to be. She seems to be getting what she wants, too. We have very long and deep conversations. She's suddenly great in bed and she actually seems to love our sexual encounters now. We have fun, and... what more could anyone want? If it's heaven, it must be heaven for her, too. She seems to be enjoying it as much as I am. We seem to have an equal desire to give to each other. I love giving her pleasure. It excites me and drives me on. The thing is, though, Grace never used to seem that interested in what I thought about things or what happened at work or especially in having sex. Now she can't seem to get enough of any of it or of me. Or is it really Grace? Maybe it's just a hallucination born out of profound loss and desire.

He sat thinking in circles. His head was spinning in a dizzying whirlpool. *I should leave it alone. I really should.* He shook his head back and forth, trying to shake the waters of frustration out of his hair after a dip in the ocean of his confusion. "Take a breath," he told himself.

Karl Otto tried to focus his attention on problems at work, but he failed miserably. His curiosity got the best of him. He decided to try to figure it all out without talking to Grace about it. "After all," he mused, "she had implied that everything was simply okay in our relationship and at work. She seemed to have no real problem with the fact that I couldn't call her on her phone and that her employer told me she was dead. Is it possible that she could be in such total denial of being dead that she continued on anyway? Is it, for that matter, possible for me to be in so much denial that I would actually conjure her up every night and on the weekends? Especially in such a vivid, tangible, and realistic way? Does she simply dematerialize at dawn?" Nothing made sense.

The next day, Karl Otto decided to go home early from work. He arrived to an empty house. Even the cat was scarce. He grabbed a beer and sat in the recliner and waited for Grace to appear. *There's that music again!* He thought as he drifted into sleep.

He awoke when he heard the garage door open and ran to the window in the door connecting the garage. She was pulling in as usual. She was surprised to see him home early. "Hi," she said. There was a lilt in her voice that sounded like genuine happiness to see him. She leaned down to pet and cooed at Algernon.

"Hi," he replied. He knew he was happy to see her, although there were serious questions lurking in the back of his mind. He grabbed her and pulled her close in his arms. Partly because he was happy to see her and partly to reassure himself that she was still real and substantial. *She feels as solid as ever!* "I don't ever want this to end," he suddenly realized he said aloud.

"End? Why did you say that? Is something wrong?"

"Not at all. I meant I want this to go on forever. I'm just so in love with you. I mean, I miss you all day. We've been doing so well lately and..."

She touched his cheek. "That's sweet. I miss you all day too, and I really believe it will never end."

What does that mean? She walked into the house and headed for the kitchen. She took out some frozen food to thaw. Karl said, "why don't you put that back and we'll go out for dinner."

She stopped and looked at him for a long time. There was puzzlement and indecision on her face. "Well, I don't know about that. I don't think we can do that."

"What do you mean?"

"Well... What if someone saw us?"

"What if they did?"

She stood stock still, staring at him in a curious way. Nothing happened in the void that lasted precisely thirty-five seconds. There seemed to be a dawn of realization on her face. She hesitated for another minute. She regained her composure and smiled. The world started up again after its momentary stall. "Let's order in tonight babe. I don't feel up to going anywhere," she said abruptly.

"Okay," he said.

They stood staring at each other for a moment. The air, puzzled by the situation, had fled the room followed by the sound. There was no movement either, only light penetrated the space between them. They stood in a tableau as though they were in a photograph, like in a movie poster. Not even the cat moved. Karl began to realize that there might be some kind of danger in pursuing this.

"We can order from that new Italian place," he said breaking out of the statuesque impasse. Grace seemed to shake clear of the paralysis too. Sound and air rushed back to fill the vacuum of indecision.

"That sounds great. I'll go change while you order."

"Oh, don't ever change," he joked; "I like you just the way you are!" He could hear snickering coming from the bedroom, but it sounded almost ironic. He frowned. Karl Otto called information and got connected to the restaurant. He ordered enough to have leftovers for two more days.

The delivery girl materialized with the food in what seemed like record time. *The restaurant is close by, and they probably have the food ready or nearly so.* He guessed it made sense. He had paid for it with credit on the phone and handed the girl a tip. They ate in silence at first. He saw Grace giving him some sidelong glances. He tried not to signal that he noticed.

What's that about? Is this a loving glance or is she studying me for some reason?

He asked her about her day at work and she told him several stories about some of the people whom he remembered he had met at some of the company functions over the years. He was puzzled. *She sounds as though she actually did go to work. Her stories didn't have any hint of fabrication. She had never been good at that.* He could only conclude that she had a life outside of the house during the day. He thought to himself, *I just visited her old office and they confirmed that she died as did my Internet search and my colleague at my office.*

He said, "It's a good thing we have the house almost paid off. Now you can put your whole paycheck away and I can take care of the bills on mine."

"That's great!" she said. But something in her voice sounded odd. There was a long silence before she spoke. She stood and walked to him and sat on his lap. "I'm so happy," she distracted.

"Me too," he echoed. "But I don't know what to do. I can't stop thinking about you, us I mean, and what's happening…"

She put a finger up to his lips and said, "Let's not talk about it right now." He kissed her finger. Long pause. "At least not yet."

Karl blinked and his head seemed to nod unconsciously. He looked at her for a long while. "I think I'm beginning to figure that out," he mumbled.

"Okay," she responded in a soft, warm voice, "I wish it was different, but I think that's the way it has to be for the present. I guess. Maybe."

"Okay. I think I can accept that," he said. "As long as I have you. That's all that matters to me. Everything else is secondary. No, everything else is unimportant."

She got up and walked a few aimless steps. She didn't seem to know where she was going. It appeared as if she was simply trying to put distance between herself and the topic. He didn't feel as though she was trying to get away from him. She seemed to want to simply change the subject.

"But," she quickly added, looking back over her shoulder, "you can go out and do things without me whenever you need to. It's really alright. In fact, I want you to. It excites me to see you happy."

"Okay," he said; "But..." She silenced him with a finger to her lips. It seemed as if she were almost kissing him by proxy. He felt it on his own lips from across the room.

He was silent for a while. *What does this mean? I know I have to hold back. She seems to know more than I do. I'm not about to risk ruining what we have.* "There is one thing that I don't understand," he said. He just couldn't seem to help himself. "I don't remember a few months of my life."

She had circled back toward him. "Shush, she said, as she put a finger to his mouth again. He kissed it again and stopped.

"I see. That's one more thing I can't talk about."

She nodded. "Not yet, anyway."

"Okay," he shrugged. "I love you and I'll do anything to keep you here with me." They sat in silence. He thought for a minute before he spoke. "Why don't you quit your job?" he repeated. "You can just stay here. There's no need for you to go anywhere now."

"I don't know..." she said, pondering the offer. "Well, maybe I could do that. I could be your house nymph! Your sex slave maybe," she said with a chuckle in her voice.

"No. I don't want a slave. I want you just the way you are. The way we are now. I want us to enjoy each other's thoughts and pleasures, and so on."

"That sounds best," she said. "But I could pretend to be a slave and do whatever you want in bed, at least sometimes," she teased. "Please?" she said with a grin signaling her humor. She giggled.

"Okay, you temptress. You're incorrigible! Who wouldn't want to have it their way? But I already have it my way. The way I want is to have you always. We're inseparable."

"I know silly, but I'd like to try it at least once. I think it would make sex more exciting sometimes because I wouldn't have to try to control anything, so I could let go totally. You know, variety! I trust you. You've never tried to hurt me."

"Well, it's your choice. You know I'd never hurt you, no matter what." He thought for a nanosecond. *Actually, slaves aren't voluntary anyway*, Karl Otto realizing the oxymoron. *Voluntary slavery. Not possible. Does she really mean that? Is she testing me?*

Karl Otto was confused. Grace had always been over-controlled and controlling, for that matter. It had been almost on the verge of paranoia. She always seemed to fear something undefinable. She was most often on guard with anxiety over trying anything new in any area of life. Now she was offering total trust and surrender to her own body, passions, and fantasies.

This is so extremely the opposite of the Grace I thought I knew. Not that I'm complaining by any stretch. True, she did sometimes have orgasms in bed, but he always suspected she had them in spite of herself. It was as if her body's desire outstripped her self-control sometimes. There were times when Karl Otto extended their love making for long periods of time on purpose, to give her emotions and sensations time to overwhelm her. Her true desires overcame her reticence. She had, in those days, no choice but to surrender to her own passions.

She seemed to be anxious about it early in their relationship but soon seemed to appreciate that her anxiety had been overcome. Once in a while. She certainly was more relaxed for an hour or so afterward until her façade returned with a vengeance. He usually knew when she was faking it, but he never let on that he knew. It was unsatisfying when she did. But now, it was all different. She seemed to have made a genuine change not just in sex, but that was the most striking. *Maybe women who are overly controlled need to let go of it sometimes to experience themselves fully. Maybe. I don't know.* He stared off at nothing in particular.

But now! Grace is loose and open to her desires and passions. She wants to talk to me and share intimate conversations. She even seems to want to take pleasure in me. And, if that's not enough, she seems to get off on pleasing me. She seems to want to please me in every way. Not just sexually. Hell, she even tried to cook! He chuckled to himself.

"What are you smiling about?" she asked.

"Oh, I was just realizing how happy I feel and the depth of love I have for you." *I'm certainly not complaining.*

She said, "You were not!" She paused and he felt her eyes staring right past his mental gymnastics. "Okay, don't tell me, see if I care." She smiled and kissed him on the forehead.

He fell asleep on his back and Algernon slept between his legs, apparently not realizing whose legs they were, under the covers.

That night, Karl Otto had a dream that he was arriving home and Grace was not there. He told himself that she had to work late and forgot to tell him. But it got very late and he started to worry. He pushed the auto redial for her cell. There was a buzzing sound and that voice message sounded again. It was distorted and garbled this time as though it too, was out of order.

He waited for a few minutes and redialed, but he got the same message. He hung up and decided he just had to wait until she came home to hear her explanation. Two more hours went by and his phone rang. It wasn't Grace's number. In fact, he surmised that it was a commercial number because it had three zeros at the end. There was always that general number and a million extensions. He hesitated to answer. It could be a sell job. *But it's too late for that.* The phone kept ringing more angrily. It seemed irritated that he didn't answer.

"Hello?"

"Is this Mr. Karl Otto?"

"Yes. Who's calling?"

"This is Dr. Cassandra at Memorial hospital. There has been an accident involving your wife. I think you'll want to come down here right away."

Karl was jolted out of his dream. He jumped. His legs kicked out. The cat was airborne, screeching like a newly launched rocket approaching the sound barrier.

Grace jumped. "What's the matter?"

"Oh, I was having one of those nightmares again."

"What was it about?"

"I really don't remember," he lied. He remembered that they shouldn't discuss these things, so he kept it to himself.

CHAPTER TWENTY-FOUR
Jeremy Therapy Nine:
John Doe Dreaming Memories

John Doe was sitting in the office alone while Jeremy went to get coffee. He looked around the office. It was shabbier and the furniture was more worn than he remembered. It was still dusty from all the problems that had blown in over the years like dead autumn leaves. John Doe thought it was worn out like a favorite old shoe that was well past the need to be discarded, but so comfortable and broken in that you were reluctant to throw it out. *It feels lived in, or was it threadbare?*

There was a picture frame on the desk. He took a peek at it. It was of Jeremy and his wife and two kids who looked to be pre-teens. He thought they probably looked happy. It was difficult to tell, they all had Jeremy's razor straight mouth that never seemed to smile or frown completely. He remembered seeing women who had Botox injections and could barely even speak with any facial expression. It looked more like a poster for Sesame Street. This was the first time he'd seen it, and it looked new. There was a price tag on the back that had been overlooked.

Maybe Jeremy had reconciled with his wife. He seemed happier than in previous sessions somehow, despite the lack of the ability to smile. His strides were a little bit longer and he seemed much lighter afoot. His eyes seemed clearer and his voice had a slight lilt as well. When Jeremy returned with the coffee, John Doe noticed the wedding ring had mysteriously rematerialized on his finger.

"So how are you?" Jeremy asked. His smiling voice was accompanied by a cheerful, but uneven sparkle in his left eye.

"I'm okay. You seem happy today, though."

"I'm alright. But what about you? How are the dreams and memories coming?"

"I did have some dreams, but not the one that keeps coming back."

"Well, can you remember enough to tell me about them?"

"Yes. Some of them, I think. They fizzle out quickly and disappear into the ether."

"Okay, why don't you tell me what you do remember before any more of them disappear?"

"I did write some down." He reached into his plastic bag briefcase and retrieved the most recent notebook and thumbed through it to refresh his memory. "I remember being chased by some men and I was scared. I don't know who was chasing me or why. This time, I was in a city and I ran down an alley, but it was a dead end. I couldn't see any way out until I saw a fire escape. I climbed it, but those guys climbed after me. When I got to the roof, there were more guys there. They must have climbed the stairs in the building. Again, I was faced with the impossible choice of death by jumping or waiting for them to kill me."

"How did you feel?"

"Scared... terrified."

"What went through your mind?"

"I thought, 'these guys are going to kill me.'"

"Did you do anything else?"

"No. The only way I could escape was to wake up."

"Wow. Did you actually decide to wake up?"

"Yeah. Now that you mention it, I think I did!"

"How did you feel when you woke up?"

"I was scared. My heart was racing and I was sweating. My bed was soaked from it, but I was relieved."

"What are you feeling right now, as you talk about it?"

"I feel some of the fear, but it's kind of in the background now. The dream was very vivid though, and it seemed so real."

"What do you make of that John? Seeming so real, I mean."

"Well, maybe you're right about these things having to do with actual memories. I don't know. The ones that keep coming back seem to be about violence, and about me being threatened and attacked."

"Okay, John. I think it may be time to take a step further. You can start following up the relaxation exercise with going back to the most remote memory you can."

"You mean back to the first time I remember? To the time when I was laying in the street?"

"Yes; but you need to be careful. Don't push it too far. If you get upset, stop and relax before you proceed. If you can't relax while you're in the memory, come back to now, and calm yourself. Open your eyes and reorient yourself to here and now while you relax in the safety of the present moment. Let's start where you left off just before you were passed out the first time after you fled."

"Okay, Doc."

"Alright, John. Let's start now, if you're up to it. I want to be sure you can do it here first before you try it alone. Do you feel up to it?"

"Sure, Doc. I'll do whatever it takes." He closed his eyes and stared at the insides of his lids. There was a red and purple haze at first before everything went completely dark.

"Alright, start by relaxing and then return to where you left off, where you left the bookmark. The pause button. Signal me if you're having trouble and need my assistance. Just raise a finger to let me know if you need my help."

"Okay, Doc."

John Doe closed his eyes and Jeremy waited. John Doe did not appear to be in much distress for about five minutes after he completed the relaxation. Jeremy saw the muscles of his shoulders tighten. He stopped and Jeremy watched him relax and start up again. This happened several times in twenty minutes. Then John Doe's finger shot up.

Jeremy said, "Alright John, I want you to listen to me closely. I'm here and you're safe. I want you to take a few deep breaths and relax. Open your eyes when you're ready."

John Doe took some deep inhalations followed by long and loud exhales that disturbed the dust particles still afloat in the atmosphere. He opened his eyes and looked around the room and at his therapist, then he sneezed. *I wonder how many patients' problems are exacerbated by their allergies.*

"Okay good," said Jeremy. "Now, begin to realize that you are here and that you are safe. Breathe and relax. Let me know when you're back here and now and feeling completely safe."

A few minutes later, John Doe said, "I'm back. I'm okay now."

"Good. I think we've done enough today. I think it would be best if you debriefed your experience today before you leave. That way I can gauge your responses, and you can put the memory in perspective of being here and now looking back objectively, rather than re-experiencing it."

"Okay, Doc; but give me a minute."

CHAPTER TWENTY-FIVE
Karl Otto: Filling the Gap

Karl Otto seemed happier than anyone at his office had ever seen him, or so they said. His secretary even asked him what was up. Did he have a girlfriend? That took him off guard. He told her no, but he was feeling better than he had in a while. His boss even praised him for his excellent work. He seemed more creative lately, and more efficient.

He and Grace continued with their nighttime life and Karl Otto continued his day job. It was increasingly clear that certain subjects were off the table if he wanted things to continue.

He remembered the old woman in his office saying he didn't belong in this world. He had wondered since childhood whether he really belonged, *but don't most kids wonder that? After all, weren't they always trying to find their own place in life? Teenagers usually feel like they're aliens in their own family.* No one seemed to understand. But he had continued to feel out of place all of his life. As a boy, he remembered, he used to look into the bathroom mirror and wonder about that left-handed Karl on the other side. *What is that world like?* It seemed to be the same as his, but that Karl seemed backward. It seemed as if the Karl on the other side moved and did everything exactly the same as he did only left-handed. *Did he think the same things too, or was his thinking the direct opposite?*

I guess that old witch must have tapped into my insecurities. Maybe we never completely get over them. Karl Otto shook his head trying to reboot reality. But he had seemed different from everyone else all his life. He picked up the office extension and called maintenance.

A deep voice said, "Maintenance."

"This is Karl Otto on the thirteenth floor. There is a cleaning lady who was up here about seven-thirty the other night. She was an older, African American woman, probably in her sixties, who had a limp. I'd like to talk to her if I could. Can you tell me when she'll be here again? She's not in trouble or anything, I just wanted to ask her a question."

There was a long silence. The voice said, "I'm sorry sir, we don't have anyone who works here that fits that description. We don't hire people with limps. It's too much of a liability for a maintenance employee. It also sounds like this person is older than anyone presently on our crew."

"Huh… could she be someone you don't know since you work the day shift and she works at night? Maybe she's a new hire?"

"No sir. I'm the one who hires everyone."

"Okaaay," said Karl Otto. "Thanks anyway." He hung up and shook his head. His brow was wrinkled, his shoulders were hunched, and he pointed his palms up while he spread his arms wide. "What the fuck!" he huffed. "I guess that's the end of that story." But he was haunted by her. He couldn't get that old woman out of his mind. She was occupying too much space in his brain for someone that didn't even exist!

Another week went by before the recurring dream of Grace's death reinserted itself into his somnolence. It was the same at the beginning, but it went further. He received the call from the hospital. But instead of jumping out of his dream, he continued it.

He rushed to the hospital and was directed to the surgical department waiting room where he sat for two hours. The surgeon, whose name he couldn't remember, came out and told him that Grace had died despite the heroic efforts they had made to save her. The shock was too much for him. He leaped out of his sleep. He kicked the covers off and the poor cat suffered again.

Grace asked, "What's going on?"

"Just another nightmare honey. I'm sorry to disturb you."

"What was it about this time?"

"I really don't remember," he lied again. "I just know it was upsetting."

"Well, I wish you could tell me about these things. I hate to see you upset so much."

"Sorry." They fell back asleep arms and legs intertwined.

When Karl Otto awoke in the morning, he saw that Grace had vanished again. He did hear the garage door open and close, but he didn't bother to get up and pursue her.

They went on every night having wonderful conversations and good food. They had settled into good sex about every other evening. His only regret was that they couldn't go out to a restaurant or a performance together, but he was willing to forgo that if it meant keeping her with him. He knew he'd have to go to some evening business functions, but he'd just be home late. He might have to travel out of town occasionally, but that would only be in rare situations.

The same nightmare came a few days later. He answered the phone and was told that Grace was in an accident and that he should rush down to the hospital. He waited in the surgical lounge again and was told that Grace had died. He sat down hard and sobbed with his hands over his eyes. He was in mid-whale when someone touched him gently on the shoulder. He looked up. He was pretty sure it was a woman, but he couldn't see who it was through his tears.

She spoke, "it's alright now Karl." Her voice sounded like his Grace. He wiped his eyes and squinted. It was Grace!

He said, "How? Why? What?"

She shushed him with her finger to his lips. "I'm sorry to leave you like this. I want to make it up to you."

"What? How can you make it up to me if you're dead?"

"Don't worry, I'll see you soon. But don't tell anyone."

"Don't tell anyone? Don't tell anyone what? That you're dead? Or don't tell anyone that you're alive?"

"No, silly. There'll have to be a memorial service after the cremation."

"Okay… I guess." He rubbed his eyes again and when he looked up, she was gone.

Karl Otto awoke suddenly, but this time the cat merely adjusted position. He wasn't kicking the covers anymore, but he had tears in his eyes and his pillow was wet. Grace was at his side in the bed. He reached over and lightly, lovingly touched her hair and kissed her on the forehead. She stirred and opened her eyes.

"Are you okay?" Her voice gurgling with sleep stuck in her throat like a rock was lodged in the stream of consciousness.

"Yeah. I'm fine," he said. "I just had a dream or a memory and I think it was about what's been happening. It was about you."

She looked frightened. Her eyes widened and her mouth dropped open. "Oh my God! Is that what your nightmares were all about? They're memories?" He opened his mouth to say something, but she cut him off. "No. Don't tell me about it!" She rolled over in the opposite direction.

"But," he began to say.

She clasped her hands to her face "No! I have a bad feeling. If you talk about it, you might ruin it!" She was frightened. "Those aren't nightmares? They're memories! Oh God!" She was almost pleading.

He was even more convinced that this might be dangerous. But how could he stop dreams? No, how could he stop dreams that are actual memories? "What am I, what are *we* going to do?"

"You may be closing the gap!" she said.

"The gap?" Karl Otto sat up. *She must mean the months between her death and now! If I remember everything that happened in those months since the accident, will what we have disappear?* "Oh shit!" he said. "There has to be something we can do."

She got up and paced the room. She was obviously thinking. Sometimes she stopped and opened her mouth, but nothing came out and she redoubled her pacing. Suddenly she said, "I've got to go. I have to think. I'll see you tonight."

She dressed in a hurry and ran to the garage and opened the garage door. She started the car and pulled out. He was watching through the connecting door. She had already pulled out and must have pushed the remote because the door started to close. As it was closing, he thought he saw her car dematerialize. He could only see from the bumper down to the driveway, the closing door blocked the rest from view. *She could have simply backed up and moved out of my sightline. It was an illusion.* Karl Otto watched as Grace was swallowed up by her world and left his behind. He was deeply perplexed. *Should I let the cards fall as they will and finally grieve her loss? But I don't want to give it up. I don't want to give her up or what we've had these past few weeks. If I give into grief, will that end it?*

It was Saturday and he didn't have to be at work today or tomorrow. He was afraid to fall asleep fearing that his dreams were memories that would push her away. He tried watching movies on the stream and drank copious amounts of black coffee between many trips to the bathroom to drain it all back out to make room for more. After a while, it seemed like the continuous river of endless caffeine. He paced around the house whenever he felt the least bit drowsy. Night was crouching nearby just over his shoulder. He could feel Morpheus stalking him. The sun was nearly set as if a veil was being pulled closed, hiding the shining face of Apollo. Karl Otto felt tired. He struggled to remain awake. He had been awake most of the previous night and now it was going on seven o'clock and Grace wasn't back.

He remembered a report that a DJ had once told his audience during a fundraiser that he was going to stay awake until he broke the record for hours without sleep. A local sleep research lab contacted him and asked to monitor him in his battle to defeat Morpheus. He agreed and they placed electrodes all over him. He tried to stay awake as long as he could. His colleagues kept giving him coffee, he exercised and paced around. He tried to talk as much as he could on air. The researchers found that he had periods of micro sleep. These were brief episodes lasting fractions of a second to a second or two. Eventually, he could resist no more and could not stop his slumber. Sleep researchers have determined that one can only stay awake for so long before drifting off. No one can stay awake forever. To top it all off, the DJ reported later that he had visions and heard music even when there was no music playing. That, to the researchers, sounded like hallucinations or dreams.

   Have I lost her already anyway? If she'd only come home. He gazed unblinking out the window. His eyelids began to sink along with the setting sun in the West. He was losing the struggle. The music of a Lyre quietly wafted into his ears as he sank to the couch.

CHAPTER TWENTY-SIX
Jeremy Therapy Ten: John Doe Remembers

"What was your experience during your memory here today, John?" John Doe had taken so long to answer that Jeremy repeated his question.

"Well Doc, I saw myself lying in the street. I was going in reverse, like you said. I saw myself get up in reverse. I went back to the street where I was unconscious and awoke backward. The guy's blow on my head from behind disappeared in reverse. The car door was only open part way. I hadn't been able to open it all the way because he was standing too close. So the first steps I had taken were toward the rear of the car; only now, I was going backward. I was backing into the car." He shook his head slowly while he tried to spin the confusing world of reverse memory back on its axis. "Still going backward, I sat back in the seat and closed the door. I rolled the window back up. The guy had the gun facing me then he walked backward away."

"Did you recognize the guy?"

"No. I never saw him before. At least, that was my reaction."

"Anything else you discovered?"

"No. I don't think so. I still don't know who I am, Doc."

"Well, you've gone a long way towards it haven't you? Let's get you calmed down, John."

"Alright, Doc."

"Start your relaxation exercise." John Doe did as he was asked and Jeremy watched and waited for an interminable ten minutes. John Doe opened his eyes and smiled. "Everything alright John?"

"Yeah, Doc." There was a long pause. "Doc, I think there's something else there."

"There?"

"Yeah, you know, it's like when you feel as if there's something on the tip of your tongue and you can't quite get hold of it?"

"I see." Jeremy paused while he thought about this. "If we try to get that vague memory in the background, it'll probably recede further, like when you go after a cat. It runs farther away. You have to wait for it or lure it to come to you. Okay, John we have to stop for now. You've come a very long way today. Let's not push it any further. Let this much soak in okay?"

"Okay, Doc."

A decision struck Jeremy without warning. "Listen, I think we should meet next week instead of waiting for two weeks. This is such a heavy revelation. I think that we need to process this sooner."

"That would be great, Doc. But I thought we couldn't meet more often than every two weeks."

"I know, but I'll take care of that. I'll even skip documenting your session if they won't approve it. But I can argue that you have a session to make up from the time you were allegedly sick, but you were really with the woman at the mall. Besides, most other people have to see the psychiatrist for meds so you aren't using up their precious money for the psychiatrist's time." They scheduled another appointment for the earliest time Jeremy had available the next week.

John Doe left the office seemingly preoccupied and Jeremy was concerned. John Doe seemed happy, but anxious, too. He hoped they hadn't gone too far, too soon. *Maybe he's just upset because he's still John Doe and doesn't yet know who he really is. He's so eager to remember it all.* Jeremy sat back in his curious desk chair and tried to install himself in John Doe's world. *What must it be like, to be middle aged and have no clue about what has happened up to now in your life?*

He tried to see if he could blank out his own past. He couldn't do it completely, but he did relax and enter an unfamiliar space tangled in a wave of wonderment that seemed to take over. He began to feel a kind of numbness creeping through his body. He felt himself beginning to drift as if his moorings had been severed and the sea had suddenly taken hold. He began to pitch and roll in the storm of his own vanishing lucidity. He felt himself being lured into the din of forgetfulness spinning feet first, then headlong into the cosmic chaos.

"Jesus!" he exclaimed to nobody there. He grabbed desperately for his sanity and used it as a lever to yank himself free from the sucking maw of his foreboding reverie.

The mouse was staring at him, the roach was still dead, and the spider was attending to two more dead flies in its web.

CHAPTER TWENTY-SEVEN
Taking Leave

John Doe left Jeremy Lincoln's office and walked out of the lobby and onto the waiting bus in front of the clinic. "Hi, John," George the bus driver said.

"Hi, George."

George always joked, "where too today sir?" as if he were a chauffeur instead of a public transportation employee. They both smiled.

"Home George!" he said.

"Yes, sir!" After a long silence, George said, "I happened to look through my side mirror last time after I dropped you off. I thought I saw you get into a car with a woman. Got a babe on the side John?" He was trying to make it light, but his expression belied his concern.

John Doe felt blindsided for a silent minute while trying to conjure up something to say. He blanched while he searched for the elusive words. "George?"

"Yeah, John?"

"I have something to tell you," he confessed. "I may not see you anymore after a week or two. I may be moving into an apartment. It's in the other direction. This might be one of my last days at the shelter. That was a case worker who picked me up to show me where it is and to gain my approval."

"Well, congrats John!" George's voice was relieved and excited simultaneously.

John Doe said, "I'll miss you, though."

"I'll miss seeing you too, but I hope all goes well for you, John."

"Yeah, but I don't know how soon I'll be moving in. There's all kinds of red tape and documents to sign. I might still see you again. I don't really know yet, but it will probably be within the next two weeks." John Doe didn't want to tell George about the recovery of his memory in case nothing came of it.

They were silent for the rest of the trip. John Doe exited the bus. It was as if they were trying on the distance they were facing to get used to the fit. The event horizon on the edge of the black hole was already upon them, sucking in everything that was between them. Nothing escaped it, not even time.

"Goodbye George. Take care!"

"See you, John," he looked away. Even though you couldn't actually call them friends in the traditional sense, George realized John was his favorite passenger. He was surprised to find a mysterious lump in his throat. "If I don't see you again, take care and good luck!" he managed to choke out.

"Thanks, George; you too." John Doe's voice seemed to quiver slightly. He liked the old guy. They waved to each other. The door closed and the bus pulled away.

George watched him exit the bus and peaked at him from his side mirror. He expected John to enter the shelter like he always did. Instead, he saw John sliding into the car beside the case worker. He wondered, *why did she pick him up again? He would have taken the bus to his new digs.* After a thoughtful pause, *why didn't she pick him up at the Community Mental Health office? Maybe he has a thing going with the case worker.*

George still felt protective of John. He had always watched out for him when he got off at the shelter. There are some unsavory characters that stay there. After all, there are nefarious reasons why some of the residents there are transient. There is great potential for mishaps.

Once, a drunk got on and started to threaten John Doe. "You're in my seat, cracker!" He was slurring and weaving back and forth.

George had accelerated quickly and then hit the brake suddenly. The drunk almost fell. He grabbed for the bar to steady himself, but missed and ended up grabbing John Doe's arm. John Doe reflexively pulled away and the man fell, but somehow was able to pull himself up by the seatback. Once he righted himself, he started yelling at John Doe with accusations of being disrespectful and trying to knock him down. He started cursing and swearing. "You dirty honkey! You pushed me down," he slurred.

John Doe tried to keep his cool, but his anxiety was soaring. He felt his blood pressure peeking through the clouds of fear. He thought his arteries were about to burst. He was in a defenseless sitting position with this big angry drunken black man, who obviously had it in for white guys, looming over him.

George pulled to the curb and stopped the bus. He rose from his driver's seat and transformed into the Hulk. John Doe thought he looked a little green and seemed to increase in size.

George was towering over the man now. He quickly grabbed him and deposited him in an empty seat. The guy spat curses through his few remaining teeth and tried to strike at George from the seat, but George blocked it and stood the man up by his collar. "That's it!" said George. He held the guy with one hand and pushed the release to open the bus door with the other. He dragged the guy off the bus and climbed back in. "Don't get on my bus again until you can behave yourself."

The door closed in the man's inebriated face just as the guy was coming back at George. John Doe heard the gears mesh and the bus lurched forward and slowly pulled away. The drunken man stumbled backward. He had been cursing the entire time and continued his ranting. His image grew ever dimmer as the bus distanced itself until he was nothing more than a shimmering mirage dematerializing into the immediate past. But his drunken ranting continued to echo in John Doe's ears. George had returned to his natural size.

"Thanks," said John Doe.

"No problem John. I can't allow violence on the bus. Jake is not so bad really, when he's sober, that is. Of course, those times are becoming fewer and farther apart. When he gets too much to drink, he no longer recognizes this planet and he loses it. To him, the Earth had transformed into an alien landscape where he's the only African-American among Caucasians, all of whom are ready to destroy him. He hates white people and blames them for his failures in life. Most of it is his own doing, but I have to admit that the establishment, mostly white society, has hurt him. All he has is a tiny welfare check and a crappy little place to live. They simply broom people like him under the rug with a few dollars and occasional rehab. He used to be a productive citizen. He has a college degree in some kind of automotive design. He says he was unfairly fired and started drinking. He said he never drank before that. It obviously made an already bad situation worse. He told me he had been discriminated against. According to him, the company apparently replaced him with three other token black men. That way, they couldn't be accused of racial discrimination. Having to replace him with three people makes me suspicious that he was doing a good job but was given more responsibility than was possible for one man to manage, no matter how good he was. He told me that he complained that it was impossible to do the work by himself. They told him he was behind and that he wasn't a team player. When he asked for help, they fired him for incompetence, but then hired three people to do the same job. But he started drinking. His life was already in the crapper, but the alcohol flushed him all the way down to the sewer of ethanol despair."

John Doe had remained silent. There was nothing to say. He just nodded and George saw his shrug in the mirror. George had remained silent too. Truth seemed self-evident.

George eventually climbed back down from his lofty flashback memories. *I really will miss John.* He smiled and shook his head. *He sure is different. He doesn't belong out here on the street.*

.

The Juxtaposition Paradox Charles R. Stern

CHAPTER TWENTY-EIGHT
Jeremy Therapy Eleven: John Doe's Revelation

"I'm starting to remember!" John Doe exclaimed. "You were right about the dreams being memories!" He hadn't even taken his usual seat in Jeremy's office yet, but the dust was already flying. Jeremy was taken by surprise and looked up abruptly. The tidal wave struck the shore and swept away even the tiniest trace of stable, rational thought.

"Really? Spill it!"

John Doe sat down with an excited plunk in the usual chair which only served to obscure the air between them. He was so wrapped up in what he was about to say that he didn't even notice that there was no padding left on the seat. The pain was overshadowed.

"Well," John Doe began. He took a minute and appeared to recapture his runaway breath. He sucked in more dust, composed himself, and recalled the memory as clearly as he could conjure it up. "I remembered that I was apparently married. At least I had a fleeting image of a woman who seemed like a wife. At least I think she was my wife. I don't know. Maybe I'm divorced. Maybe she was an ex-wife. She was good looking, though."

Jeremy was on the edge of his seat. "Was there anything else?"

"Yeah, there was." There was a momentary silence while he tried to pull back the memory before it sank back into oblivion. "I thought that I could retain it longer if I told you about it. If I said it aloud to someone," he continued.

"I no longer think there is anyone after me. I think I was carjacked. I don't know yet who I am, but, as you know, I remember the guy coming up to me in the car with the gun. He told me to get out. I did as he asked, but getting out of the car I had turned slightly toward the rear of the vehicle. That's when he hit me on the back of the head. I was unconscious for a while. I guess it was a while because there was no one around when I awoke. The thing is, just before the incident, I remember that I seemed to have taken a wrong turn and ended up in an unfamiliar area. It didn't occur to me that anyone was after me. So I naively opened the window thinking the guy needed help. I was surprised when he pulled the gun on me. That's why I think that it was a simple carjacking that went wrong!"

Jeremy was elated. "That's great John! You must be relieved."

"Oh man, am I!"

"Fantastic! I'm so glad for you." There was a pause for a moment before Jeremy continued. The gears of realization had begun to speed up and his mind raced ahead of him. After he caught up to himself, he said, "Do you think our little exercises of relaxation and attempts at memory recovery helped? "Jeremy was trying unsuccessfully to conceal his hopes that he had been of assistance.

"Oh yeah, Doc! No doubt about it! I was doing the exercise this morning when I remembered this much. I'm so relieved that I don't have to worry about someone stalking me or hurting me. I think it was a simple carjacking gone wrong. At least it went wrong for me. I don't know what happened to the carjacker." There was another pause while thoughts flooded in and penetrated his conscious mind.

"I think what happened was simply a run of the mill carjacking. I think the carjacker was afraid that I was going to go off on him. I was pretty mad and I let him know it. I was yelling at him and he probably thought I might call attention to myself and what he was doing. I think he said, "Shut up asshole!" just before he hit me. I should have kept my mouth shut. It was stupid."

"That's incredible! Congratulations, John."

"Thanks, Doc, but who am I? I still haven't a clue."

"Well, you'll probably start to remember that too, now that you've made it through the worst of the trauma."

"Well, Doc, I hope you're right."

"I think so, John." There was a long anticlimactic pause while Jeremy's brain suddenly halted in its tracks and his conscious mind finally caught up and slammed into the stalled train of thought. "John?"

"Yeah, Doc?"

"I wonder." He was hesitant to say more but felt compelled to do so. "Well John, I was thinking. What would you say if we go to the press and ask one of the news stations to broadcast your picture around the entire region? Someone is bound to see it and recognize you. Now that you're not fearful of being pursued, the press can circulate your picture. Someone is likely to see it and recognize you. Once you are reunited in your usual environment, you'll probably remember the rest of it."

"Great idea Doc; let's try it." John Doe suddenly had second thoughts. The dust began to settle in his brain. "On the other hand Doc, I don't know. I've been afraid to do things like that for so long now."

"Yes I know, but that was when you were afraid someone was trying to find and kill you. Now you know that it was a carjacking."

"That's true…"

"Well, think about it, John. When someone recognizes you, you'll be reunited with friends and family. That should hasten your recovery. All of your memories will probably return more quickly."

"I suppose you're right, Doc. I would like to get back to my normal life, whatever it was." A long, pensive pause ensued. John Doe was lost for a few minutes in a silent morass of tangled ruminations and misgivings mixed with hope. "Okay, Doc. Let's do it."

"Alright John, I'll call a reporter I know, if that's alright with you."

"I guess so, Doc. This is all happening so fast."

"I'm sorry John. I don't want you to do anything you're against or that you don't feel comfortable with."

John Doe was silent for a long time. Gears turned and sparks ignited before calm descended over him. "I've been in a hurry for so long and suddenly I'm hesitant! To be honest with you, Doc. I think I'm afraid of finding out who I was. What if I wasn't a good person in my previous life?"

"John, do you think you've been a good person since you lost your memory?"

"Yeah. I guess so, Doc; yeah."

"Well, what makes you think you were otherwise before this fate smacked you on the head?"

"I see what you mean, but it is scary."

"I can't imagine what you're going through right now John, but take time to think about it. If you don't want to do it that way, we'll continue to take one slow step at a time just like we've been doing all along. You'll probably remember it all eventually anyway.

John Doe sat in Jeremy's silent office for the longest five minutes of his known life and wandered through the labyrinth of possible scenarios and probable misfortunes. "Okay, Doc."

"Okay?"

"Yeah. I thought it through. I've come this far and, like you say, I'll eventually remember anyway. Why not see if we can accelerate it? Besides, I'm tired of living in shelters and taking busses everywhere. Apparently, I owned a car in my real life. I'm going to be a janitor now and I have the feeling that I had a better job or at least I'm probably capable of more than that. Besides, I'll have a chance to repair the damage, if there is any. Let's go for it, Doc."

"Alright John, but you can back out any time you want."

"Okay Doc, but I don't think I will."

The Juxtaposition Paradox   Charles R. Stern

CHAPTER TWENTY-NINE
Jeremy and the Team

Jeremy was excited about the breakthrough with John Doe. He waited until Dr. Suiminski asked about the case. He told him about John Doe's memories and that it appeared to be a breakthrough. There was a discussion about it and Dr. Suiminski asked about the next step. Jeremy explained that John Doe wanted to go to the media to help him reconnect with his family and friends. He said that he knew of a news reporter who can help.

Dr. Suiminski said, "Don't you think that it goes beyond the therapeutic boundaries?" He usually put his criticism into a question so others would appear to come up with their own idea that, no surprise, matched his.

Julie Harper was, of course, the doctor's Greek chorus; always taking a supporting position, but with much more gusto. "You should probably leave it all up to Mr. Doe. Don't you think?"

Jeremy didn't hear much of what she said because she had transformed into a snarling dog. Jeremy tried not to respond with defensiveness. "Well, I understand your point of view, but all I am going to do is introduce John and the reporter. They can do the rest." He was ignoring Julie Harper and looking right through the doctor.

"Well," said Dr. Suiminski, "please keep the clinic out of it and don't agree to be interviewed." He was uncharacteristically direct. It was probably because he feared he would be held responsible as the supervising psychiatrist if anything went wrong.

The room got brighter for a moment until Julie started barking again. "You know, while it may not be illegal, it's probably unethical to do that. She was voicing the good doctor's fears.

"Unethical?" asked Jeremy. "You mean that simply introducing John Doe to the reporter, the very thing he wants, is unethical?" He was trying to hold back his irritation without complete success.

"Well, it seems like it. Besides, even if it wasn't unethical, isn't it counter-therapeutic?"

"Counter therapeutic? How is that possible?" Jeremy shot back with irritation. *Counter therapeutic?* He thought. *She really is pulling out all the rods in the reactor. Was there going to be a meltdown or an explosion? A China syndrome?*

"Well, it interferes with his ability to make independent decisions."

"Well, it seems to be his decision, and I told him that he doesn't have to do it and that he could back out of it at any time." Jeremy was nearly out of breath from spewing counter venom.

"Well, maybe he's just agreeing to what you want him to do." Julie was getting more strident. Jeremy began to see that she was competing with him for who is the most correct about therapeutic approaches for the attention of Dr. Suiminski.

"Look," he said, trying to curb his irritation. "John Doe's entire therapeutic goal has been to recover his memory and his identity in the process. He has been doing that and this will most likely help him make further progress toward it. So if I do a simple thing to assist him in making contact with a community resource, isn't that what we do on a regular basis? Isn't that what you do as a social worker?" He stared and pointed his chin at Julie Harper then he paused for effect before he charged ahead.

"For instance you, Julie, gave him a bus pass and helped him get the food card. You have been getting him in touch with resources for a job and a place to live. Those are community resources are they not? So why is this so different? It's up to him to follow through with them. It's the same in this situation." Everyone was silent.

"I know you probably think I may be too close to John Doe to be objective." He was trying to curtail her next move in the game by making it first. "This simply makes sense. He'll more than likely reach his goal on his own now, once he's exposed to his former life. I see nothing wrong with that."

Julie Harper spoke up, "but you have to consider the boundaries."

"Boundaries?" said Jeremy cutting her off. "There will be none once he has hooked up with his family and his previous life. He won't even come here anymore."

Julie opened her mouth, but nothing emerged. She was uncharacteristically dumbstruck. She looked at Dr. Suiminski for rescue, but he was at a loss, too.

There was a vacuum of silence in the room until Dr. Suiminski said, "okay. I see your point, but we can't have any other involvement than to give him resources. If that happens to be the media, so be it." He thought for a moment and everyone hung suspended waiting for his next pronouncement. "We have to be very careful not to risk losing our funding over even a hint of impropriety." Now he donned his administrator hat.

Jeremy said, "forgive me for saying this, but from a political and funding point of view, this might just be a great human interest feather in our cap when the funding agency discovers our role in reuniting an amnesic patient lost for around a year, with his family."

"I see your point," Dr. Suiminski said. "Alright. I don't see any harm in it. Go ahead with the plan. Just be careful."

"Okay. I will." Jeremy gave a sidelong glance at Julie Harper, who was so slumped down in her chair that, given her miniscule stature, made her nearly invisible below the eye level of the table top.

CHAPTER THIRTY
Karl and Grace: Experiments

Karl Otto felt someone tugging at him. "Karl! Wake up!" The voice sounded far away. He wasn't able to climb out from the depths of the well. He couldn't rise above the twilight of consciousness and remained in the border between dream and reality. He had struggled against sleep and lost to Morpheus. Now he was pulled in two directions by the God of sleep and that voice pulling at him from far above. He was a rubber band being stretched in opposite directions waiting to see toward which one he'd eventually snap. One end was stuck fast in quicksand and the other end was pulling hard to extract him.

Whoever was attached to that distant voice helped him to his feet. He was staggering with help. He just couldn't wake up. He had forced himself to stay awake for so long that he had no choice but to sleep. At one point, he had met sleep head-on. He felt as though he was falling into a vat or something.

He thought he was still dreaming. It seemed as if he was being lifted and dragged. Then he felt pushed or dumped. He felt the back of his head hit something before everything went black. *This dream is really weird,* he thought as he slipped off again. *There's actual pain.*

He awoke feeling as though his body was being bounced around. He finally won the struggle to open his eyes and realized that he was in the backseat of a car covered up by some blankets. The road was full of potholes and caused the car to bump and grind. He felt terror. *What's happening? Where am I? Where am I being taken?* He yelled, "Hey! What's happening? Who's there? Where are you taking me? Help!" He was still paralyzed with sleep and succubus was still sitting on his chest.

He felt the car slowing and then the sound of gravel before coming to a stop. He felt terror and crouched the best he could manage, ready to spring out at his captors, if necessary. The driver's door opened and someone was walking on the gravel. The back door opened with a jerk. Someone was pulling the covers off. It was Grace! "Karl, it's me, Grace, are you alright?"

"Well, I've been better," he managed to gurgle. Karl Otto struggled to climb out of the car. He felt stiff and sore. The ride had been brutal. He was unsteady and reached for the car to maintain his balance. "What the hell is happening? Why did you put me in the car?"

"I couldn't risk anyone seeing you and you were so deeply asleep that I couldn't wake you."

"You wanted to hide me? Why? Are you planning to get rid of me? What were you planning to do with me?"

"No, no, no! Karl, wake up! You don't really understand what's happening at all do you?"

"I have no idea. All I know is that you died and there must have been a memorial service after the cremation and you have been with me ever since. Well, no, I only know that you've been with me every night in the past couple of months. There is a gap of several months in my memory." He stood staring at Grace in silence for a moment waiting for the clouds to part and allow the moonlight to penetrate his brain. "That's all I know." The moon went into hiding again.

The Juxtaposition Paradox   Charles R. Stern

She shook her head and shrugged. "We have to get you home and hidden for now. I'll explain later. Get in."

"In the back seat?"

"No dummy. In the passenger seat but, you'll have to duck down near the house so no one will see you. It's late and it's not likely anyone will notice, but we can't risk it."

"Okay, I guess." Karl became aware of a pain on the back of his head. He reached up and felt a bump and when he looked at his hand there was a little blood. "Except for this. Did you hit me on the head?"

She saw the blood on his hand. "Oh my God! How did that happen? I'd never do that to you, Karl." She glanced in the car and there was a metal rolling carry-on case on the back seat. She sometimes used it for rare a business trip. "You must have hit your head on the sharp edge of my travel case in the back seat. I'm so sorry Karl." She felt terrible, but she also had urgency in her voice.

Karl Otto looked around and recognized the area and that it wasn't too far from their home.

"Come on! Get in. We have to get home." He got in as directed. As they pulled away, a raccoon stepped out into the road and watched them disappear into the fog of early morning. He shrugged, shook his head, crossed the road, and disappeared into the brush.

They drove the three miles or so to the house. Karl dropped down dutifully for the last mile. He still felt woozy from sleep and the inadvertent blow to his head. The world was spinning inside his concussion and he felt faint on and off during the ride. He was getting nauseous, too.

Grace activated the garage door remote. It opened and she pulled in and shut the door behind them.

They stepped out of the car and she went in with staggering Karl dutifully trailing behind. Karl's vertigo was diminishing, but he was a little unsteady. He felt the walls encroaching on him with foreboding. He felt something sinister lurking. His head was awash with his habit of asking recursive questions. He often made himself dizzy with puzzlement. *What's happening? Why would Grace kidnap me, her own husband, merely to return me from where she took me in the first place?*

As Karl Otto entered the house, he noticed some subtle differences in the landscape right away. He saw that there was a mountain of dishes and pans piled in the sink and the foothills of mail were three times the volume he remembered, and the junk mail he threw out was still there. The living room was messy with mounds of magazines and leftover cups of deserted coffee despite the fact that, just yesterday, he had straightened up.

He went over to the pile of mail and started to sort through it. Grace rushed over and reached for it, but he pulled away and lifted it high over his head. She said, "Karl! Don't!"

He turned his back to her and sorted through it. He was standing by the sink and shucked the junk mail and bills into it. He found the funeral home bill and the insurance documents as well as the envelopes with, he assumed, the death certificate and the police report. He pulled out the envelope with the death certificate.

In a fit of anger, he turned on Grace, who was standing there before him sobbing. He felt angry and opened his mouth to say something, but his rage quickly abated. After all, no matter what crazy thing she did, he still loved her very much. He said, still in a firm voice, "Explain this!"

"Look at it Karl," she sobbed.

He looked down and read the death certificate. It had his name on it! It said *he* had died! "Oh my God!" He felt weak and stumbled to the kitchen chair and dropped down with a thud. *I'm supposed to be dead now too?* "What fresh Hell is this?" He quoted Dorothy Parker

Grace came over to him and placed her hand on his shoulder. "Baby, come into the living room and sit down on the comfortable couch. I'll explain what I think I've figured out so far."

They did as she suggested. Karl followed her into the living room like Algernon, who was curiously trailing behind. He sat down hard with an audible *plop* on the couch. He sagged and soon slumped over while Grace sat cross-legged on the opposite end of the couch facing him. She leaned forward with her hands prayerfully clasped between her knees. "Karl... You died in a car crash, here where I live, and it seems that I died in the same one somewhere else, wherever it is that you live."

"Here? There? What are you talking about?"

"When you died, I went into deep mourning and isolated myself for months. I missed you and I kept thinking about how much I had actually loved you and how self-involved I had been. I realized how well you took care of us and how hard you worked. I realized that I had become depressed after the kids were off in college, especially because they were both a thousand miles away and couldn't come home very often." She was sobbing so hard now that, with her head buried in her hands, he saw the mascara soaked tears running down her face and arms. Her body started to convulse and her sobbing increased in volume and it was obvious that she couldn't talk through them. She was gasping for air in her attempt to gather the resources within her to go on.

His frustration and irritation dissolved when he witnessed the love of his life in such distress. He stood up and walked over and sat down next to her. He wrapped his arms around her and hugged her tight; until her sobs diminished to mild tremors. "I'm sorry baby," he said.

After she calmed down enough to speak, Grace looked up at him. "I isolated myself partly out of grief, but something else happened."

"Something else?" Karl was puzzled.

"Months after your death, I had to go downtown to pick up your remains from the crematorium. I was sad but didn't think too much of it at the time. When I left the garage, I thought I heard something odd as I pulled the car out. I couldn't put my finger on it at the time. It sounded like a harp or something. I think I've heard it somewhere before. I had a kind of shiver of fear like you get when you enter an unfamiliar place where danger could be lurking. At the time, I told myself that it was just because I had been isolated and cooped up in the house for so long. But now I wonder about it." She hesitated for what seemed to Karl Otto a very long time.

"It felt odd too, when I entered the place where I was supposed to pick up your remains. It was on the basement level. I took the old rickety elevator down and entered the office. I asked for the remains, but they said they searched their records, but they couldn't find any trace of your ashes, but they had some in the name of Grace Otto! I was stunned and left that place and drove home. I left my ashes there.

"All the way home I was in a panic. Here I was alive and there were ashes with my name on them! I tried to understand it. Did they get our names mixed up? Was I really dead and in some kind of Limbo? I was so confused. Maybe it was just a vivid dream.

"I was so upset and preoccupied with my demise and yours that I didn't even notice that something seemed oddly different. I started cooking a simple dinner for myself. You were no longer here to cook and I thought it would be good for me to start cooking for myself. I had been living on nuked leftovers and deliveries of pizzas and sandwiches. As you know, I'm not a good cook. I was standing at the stove stirring the goulash concoction I had cobbled together. It was awful, even though I tried to follow a recipe. I did have to substitute some ingredients, though. I was appreciating your cooking at that point and it made me miss you more. Even the bare stove screamed out *Karl!*" She was searching for the right words.

"I was wishing so hard that you were here so I could give you the same intense attention and love that you had given the kids and me. I realized how aloof I had been and I regretted being so distant for so long. I felt the tears starting to breach the dam.

"I had decided to cook," Grace continued. "I don't know why or what possessed me to do that. I rarely cooked and never really liked it. I felt pretty much the same way about cleaning. Maybe I was channeling my mother. Whenever she was upset, she'd cook a feast. I think it distracted her. In fact, she did all of the cooking and I never learned to do much of it beyond the basics. Anyway, I looked for food to cook and there wasn't much in the fridge so I combined things to make a goulash. It wasn't turning out very well, but I needed to try.

"While I was flavoring the food with salty tears, I realized how much you have always done for me, for us. The kids and me. I didn't clean very often. Not like you did. You rarely complained even though you worked so hard and such long hours on your job. I realized that I had taken you for granted while you were alive. I began to appreciate you and my love was rekindled. I actually missed you sexually. I hadn't felt like that in many years. I always loved you. I realize now that I couldn't seem to show it very well. But you were gone. I think the kids had been the center of our lives and we stopped focusing on each other.

"I was standing there; stirring the awful food I had thrown together that day not knowing whether I could stomach it. I felt like a failure at everything in our marriage. I was wishing you were still here. Just then I heard the garage door open and close. I froze. Who could that be? "I was terrified. I thought someone had gotten your garage opener from the car after you died in the accident and was breaking in. I wiped my tears on a paper towel and grabbed a knife from the drawer ready to defend myself." Her body stiffened and her hand grabbed an invisible weapon as if she had slipped back in time and re-entered the experience.

After a moment lost in the reverie, she regained the present. "Then I heard your voice calling me." Her eyes welled up with tidal pools of tears. She sniffed back the flood and struggled to compose herself.

"I wondered if I was hallucinating. Did I magically wish you back? Had I just awakened from a dream? I didn't know what to do so I tried to act normally. I dropped the knife and tried to nonchalantly stir the pot. I was struggling to keep myself from running to you. I thought you would be too shocked if I did. Besides, for months I thought, no, I knew you were dead! You went into the living room and called for me. I answered that I was in the kitchen. When I saw it really was you, I was overwhelmed with joy and love. I felt enormous relief. But I was confused. I should have been scared, but for some reason I wasn't. I was confused and intrigued instead. I wanted to please you. I hadn't felt that way in many years and I don't think I had ever felt it as intensely as I did at that moment. I shut off the stove, took off the apron, and tried to show you as much loving as I could. I just wanted to pleasure you like I never had. I looked you over and touched you to make sure you were real."

Karl Otto said, "Well you certainly accomplished that!"

"I thought I'd have an orgasm just standing there," she said through a wet smile blinking back the waterfall.

"Me too!" he blurted. His eyes were pouring now, too.

"It really was you," she said. "I was shocked, but I tried not to react. You acted as though you were surprised to see me cooking, but I could tell that you were trying to hide your shock. We had a great time that night and I wanted it to go on and on." She thought back for a moment to clarify her memory in her own mind before she went on.

She extricated herself from him and the couch. She paced around the room with the curled index finger of her right hand between her teeth. Then she abruptly halted. "I saw my death certificate later," she said. Her shoulders dropped into the slump of exhaustion and relief that one feels after a satisfying confession.

"I hadn't looked through the mail. I rarely did. I had simply retrieved it from the mailbox and put it on the kitchen counter as usual, but later, when you were asleep for an hour or so, I got up to go to the bathroom. I decided to look at it because your death certificate was there and I was puzzled about what was happening. I didn't understand how you had been alive in bed next to me and dead simultaneously. I looked through the mail and it confirmed my death! It was then that I knew I was dead. I just sat there in the kitchen for what must have been an hour. I couldn't figure out why I seemed to be alive. I couldn't figure out why I thought you were dead. The same mail I had opened before had said *you* were dead! Was I a ghost? Were you a ghost? Were we both dead and trapped in some limbo? I was struck numb. I decided to continue as if nothing had happened. I wasn't sure, but I had the feeling that talking about it might ruin it."

There were trickling tears punctuating a frightened silence before she could manage any further discussion. She finally swallowed and choked back the anxious lump that had welled up in her throat. "We had been having such intimate and honest conversations before you died... or before I died? Anyway, I wanted you so bad!" Grace said. "Our love making was incredible that night too! I had never experienced it that way before. Maybe I wouldn't let myself let go like that until then. And you were so caring and attentive to me."

"It was wonderful," he agreed. "I felt that we were growing close again," he continued, "but I was confused whether you were dead."

"I felt the same way," she said. "Closer than ever." She paused. He paused. The entire house was silent. Even Algernon sat staring at them stock still from the corner with rapped anticipation.

"I went to the couch and woke you. I got ready for work as though nothing had happened and left. It was very difficult for me to leave you now that I had you back." Another silent pause consumed her. "I figured something out, though."

"What?" he asked with intense interest. He sat up and moved to the edge of the seat.

She sat down in the overstuffed chair across from him. "After I left the house for work, it wasn't long before I realized that I had forgotten something and returned home. But when I came in, you weren't there and the house seemed different even though I had left the house just a short time before. There were leftover food dishes in the kitchen sink. The pot wasn't on the stove from the night before. I looked at the mail and death certificate said that you were dead, not me." She paused for a long minute.

"I went on to work, but I couldn't do much work. I was worried about my sanity. When I returned that night, the place was clean and orderly and the pot was in the sink. The odd thing was that I had heard that music again when I was about to enter the garage that night. I thought it might have been my phone, but when I checked it, there were no messages. I heard that music again at other times too," she said.

Karl Otto's brow wrinkled before his eyebrows shot up. He pondered this for exactly one second that seemed to drag on for much longer. "I hear it too sometimes, mostly when I go to sleep."

Grace continued, "I went to work thinking I had dreamt the whole thing, but when I returned that night I had heard that music again just before I opened the garage door. I almost felt like it was calling for me. There we were, together again." Grace thought for a minute. "Maybe we can go on this way. But I don't fully understand what it is and what if, for some reason, we can no longer crossover between these two... whatever this is. Two worlds... or dimensions... dreams...hallucinations... or... I don't know," she said. "Hades maybe?" she thought for a minute.

"I realized that you didn't understand even the little I had discovered. I started to realize that it might have something to do with your dreams." Pause. "Another thing was odd. I noticed that you were sleeping on the opposite side of the bed than you usually did and there were other things that were different."

"I always slept on that side of the bed," he interrupted.

"Not in my lifetime, you didn't. I noticed that you are right handed. You used to be a lefty."

He thought for a time before he spoke. "There was that music. You said that you heard it too. I thought it sounded like that harp-like instrument we heard at the museum last year. I think it was a lyre."

"Oh yeah," she said, "now that you mention it, I remember that. I think the docent said it was the instrument of the Greek mythical figure Orpheus. I think she said that he could charm people and animals and even stones with his music. I think she also said that he played it to charm his lover back from the dead."

"So," he said, "there's something about that music, sleep, and dreams, maybe the garage."

She rose up and paced around the room again munching mindlessly on her hungry fingers, searching for a solution. "I shushed you not to talk about it at first when you started telling me about your dreams and that they seemed to be memories; I worried that, if you remembered those empty months since the accident, the spell, or whatever it was would be broken and we'd be lost to each other forever."

Karl said, "yea, what if it stops? What if, for whatever reason we can't keep on this way?" The lights dimmed, thinking became labored, and the universe held its breath. They were silent for a long time dreading the idea that their life together would be torn apart again just when they were beginning it anew.

"Well," she said, "we seem to be able to be together in both of our..." She stalled for a minute and abruptly changed the subject. "The question is, what is going on and what are we going to do now? Are we dead or alive? Are we in a mutual dream or something? I don't know." Grace hesitated briefly.

"Whatever is happening, what are we going to do?" he asked.

"I don't know what to call this. We just have to figure out what to do next. We can't keep going back and forth between these scenes, whatever they are. Probably. Maybe?"

CHAPTER THIRTY-ONE
John Doe Advertised

Jeremy Lincoln sat opposite John Doe in his office. Somehow, he couldn't comprehend how the physical distance between them seemed to widen despite the fact that the chairs were the exact same number of inches apart. He could tell this by the deep indents in the floor where the chairs made their marks on the world from the countless cue of decades of patients and the weight of their tribulations. The room expanded in relativity. Like Dr. Who's Police Box; it was larger inside than out. It puzzled him since it seemed to Jeremy that their therapeutic rapport had actually strengthened over the time they had spent together.

Maybe it is simply an omen of some kind. But then, he didn't really believe in that sort of thing. Or did he? He wasn't sure of anything anymore. Still, the office space was expanding, so far as he could determine. As the gap between them expanded, he felt something welling up in his gut. He felt the urge to yell across the gulf that separated them.

"John," Jeremy said in a small distant voice, "I called my reporter friend. His name is Jack Walker. He anchors the evening news. He's down the hall waiting to be introduced to you. I forbade his eager cameras from coming here, but he'll talk to you for a bit now and arrange a formal interview at the station tomorrow, if that's alright with you."

"Okay, Doc. I've made up my mind to do it so let's get it over with."

"Alright, John. Just relax for a minute and I'll get Jack."

With that, Jeremy rose, the door opened to the hallway and he skated out. There was the loud banging of footsteps that felt to John Doe like gunshots cracking in his ears. His face winced with every shot. The sound of a doorknob turned and another door opened. Some muffled talking drifted back to John Doe in a firm dry wind that swept through the room. Two pairs of exploding feet were approaching. He began to realize that the blasts were actually coming from beating of his own heart.

The silhouettes of Jeremy and the figure of another man materialized in the doorway. "John Doe, this is Jack Walker. Jack this is John."

John Doe found himself standing and before he knew it, his hand was reaching out cataleptically suspended in the space between them. "Happy to meet you John!" said Jack. He flashed a blinding smile of obviously over whitened teeth that increased the lighting in the room. This was trailed by a flamboyant flourish. *I bet those teeth glow in the dark.* He kept it to himself.

He proffered a vigorous double palmed handshake that, John Doe thought, was a little too glad-handing. John Doe detected a less than substantial foundation lurking beneath the veneer of the ostensibly firm handshake. A house of cards teetering on collapse in the slightest breeze of criticism. John Doe smiled and said, "likewise Jack." John Doe shook those hands as tightly as they were presented to him. He looked Jack square in those dark and empty eyes. *Not much in there.*

There was an imperceptible shudder that traveled from Jack's brain down to his fingertips and into those of John Doe. Jack pulled back his grip just a tad too quickly from the rippling shock of their silent confrontation. Jack apparently realized on some level that his facade had been penetrated.

They sat down and the door closed. Jeremy turned and said, "Do you mind if I stay or would you rather talk to Jack in private?"

"No. Stay. Please." John Doe wanted a witness. It's difficult to trust this blank and very empty vessel.

Jack asked the standard questions you'd expect. "How did you end up in the clinic and what do you remember so far?" They talked about the things Jack would ask John Doe in the recorded interview the next day at the studio. In the end, they shook hands again, more briefly this time. Jack was more careful to cover his empty insecurities and John Doe tried to avoid eye contact. Both men smiled and Jack left the building. Jeremy chatted with John Doe briefly, reminding him to practice his relaxation routine to reduce the jitters of being interviewed on the stream.

The next day, a limousine was dispatched from the studio to transport him. The interview went well. John Doe felt a little nervous but tried to remember to do his relaxation routine just before. This helped him float through the murky waters of media distortions and correct the attempts to overly sensationalize his story. The interview lasted about a half hour, but the actual edited broadcast lasted exactly thirty seconds. It was scheduled to repeat for two days on every newscast. Of course, his corrections to their distortions were removed and the residue of sensationalism emerged from the bottom of the barrel. Calls started coming in from a suburban town about thirty-five miles outside of the city.

The Juxtaposition Paradox Charles R. Stern

CHAPTER THIRTY-TWO
A Husband and Wife Reunion

John Doe's wife heard her phone beckoning her. The ring heralded its importance. She never understood why she always knew this. There was certainly no scientific evidence that an electronic device sounded any different than any other time it rang. But her mother and her grandmother seemed to have the same sixth sense. She felt anticipation mixed with a sense of trepidation. She found herself holding the phone to her ear. "Hello?"

The voice identified himself as a news reporter from the local station. He asked, "How do you feel about your husband being found?"

There was a long empty calculated silence. "Who is this? This is not funny. My husband is dead. You should be ashamed of yourself!" She was yelling now. "What do you think you are doing? Goodbye!"

She was about to hang up when the reporter said, "No! Don't hang up! This is no joke. I thought you'd have found out by now. Your husband isn't dead. I'm... I'm..." the reporter stammered, trying to keep her on the phone. He sounded desperate. She could feel the sweat pouring off his forehead. He was drowning in his own anxiety. "I'm just trying to get the story. I work for News Corp."

"News Corp? What story? My husband has been gone for nearly a year!"

"No, no, ma'am. Oh God, you really don't know, do you?"

"Know what?"

"Your husband is alive and well."

"What are you talking about?"

"Haven't you been watching the news? Hasn't anyone called you about it? Surely someone has seen it and called you. We've been getting hundreds of calls to the station from your friends and neighbors. He has been found!"

"Found? Found? What do you mean?"

"He was carjacked and in the scuffle he was hit on his head. He has had amnesia since then. That is, until now."

She was silent for a long contemplative moment working out what to say. "I have had the phone turned off," she mumbled, "and I haven't checked the messages. I haven't been watching the stream for days either. In fact, I haven't watched it hardly at all in months. I only just turned on the phone moments before you called. I just got home from work and I haven't had time to check the messages." She suddenly felt far away until the reporter's voice brought reality crashing back with a vengeance.

"Well, ma'am, we here at News Corp have been getting lots of calls since we put his picture and the clip of the interview with him on the news broadcast. In fact, his interview was aired on the stream today. Actually..." She felt him checking the time. "It's about to go on again right now."

She picked up the remote and switched on the stream. Soon, his picture appeared followed by an interview. She screamed at the reporter, "It is him! Oh my God! I thought he was dead!"

"We'd like to reunite you as soon as possible. Can you come into the city and meet him on the air at the studio?"

"Oh, Jesus yes! I'll leave right now. I can't believe... How could this be? It's impossible! Let me find a pen. Give me the address of the studio."

"That won't be necessary. There's a limo on its way to pick you up as we speak."

"Oh my God! I have to get ready. I have to shower and change clothes and put makeup on. How long before the limo gets here?"

"Well, it's rush hour so it'll probably take forty-five minutes to an hour longer, but the driver will wait for you if you need more time. We are going to record the reunion, but the initial meeting will be broadcast live today and it will be edited as a cut-in for special broadcasts later."

She hung up without saying goodbye and turned in precisely three circles before she hurried off to the shower that she barely remembered taking. In fact, she only knew she had showered because her hair was damp. She dried her hair, brushed it, and fixed her makeup. She picked out an appropriate dress and purse. Her heart was pounding and her hands were trembling. She felt frightened. After all, she had already set in motion the life insurance claim.

She answered the phone several times. Once after her shower and, or so it seemed, between donning each article of clothing. There were numerous calls from friends, coworkers, and colleagues, but she was only half listening. They told her that they had seen her husband on the news stream earlier. Some of them had called the station and gave the reporters her address and telephone number. She finally had to stop answering the calls to finish getting ready. She knew that the reporter was going to ask her questions about her reaction and the events of the past ten months or so. She had to anticipate their questions and prepare her answers. She knew from past interviews she had participated in for her company and associated legal cases for which she had been deposed that she could simply say "I don't know" or "I don't remember" to any question, if necessary, rather than cause misunderstandings.

She discovered that she was nearly ready when the limousine pulled up. She grabbed her purse and jacket. She found a pad of paper and a pen to take with her. She reckoned it would take at least an hour to get to the studio, and longer, if rush hour was still ensconced in the freeway magically turning it into a parking lot. She could write down her thoughts on the way. She had already formulated some of them in the shower, but she wanted them to be well organized and she didn't want to forget anything.

She hurried out to the limo carrying her purse and the jacket she hadn't had time to put on. The driver stood at the ready with the door open. He shut it after her and walked quickly around to the driver's door and got in. He pulled away and drove as close to the speed limit he could, despite the remnants of rush hour traffic.

The landscape rushed past unnoticed, despite the fact that she was staring out the window for the first five minutes of the ride. The driver said, "Congratulations ma'am. You must be happy to discover that your husband is alive. I saw the preliminary report on the news earlier." She looked up at the reflected eyes beaming at her in the rearview mirror.

He had startled her back from that blank space wherever that was and made her realize her intention to prepare for the interview. She said, "thank you." She paused before she continued. "I'm sorry. I don't mean to seem rude, but I need this time for my thoughts, to prepare me for what to say when I get there."

"Okay, ma'am. I understand. I'll give you privacy. Just push the intercom button there if you need to talk to me for any reason."

"Okay, Thanks."

"No problem ma'am. It's my job." The glass partition rose separating her from his world. She wrote some ideas and comments on her paper. It helped to write them down and hear them rehearsed aloud while imagining the reporter's questions. She felt at times that she was actually there in the studio. She knew the reporter from watching the evening news so she saw him sitting there with her.

The limo pulled up to the studio just as she was emerging from her reverie.

There was a crowd surrounding John Doe when her limo approached the entrance. She rushed through the throng to him and embraced him. The security guards ushered them into the broadcast room. Makeup professionals attended them briefly, to cut down on the highlights shining from their faces, accommodating the needs of the cameras, and totally wrecked her makeup. They had hugged briefly, but John Doe still didn't seem to recognize her. He acted awkwardly and she looked hurt. At least that is the way the reporters characterized it later in their broadcasts and on social media.

Jack, the anchorman, sat them down in the interview chairs opposite his while microphones were being affixed to their clothes. He told them that they would be live soon and that their initial reunion a few minutes ago in the lobby would air first and then they would be interviewed live. That interview would be edited and rebroadcast several times during the news today and tomorrow. They would follow-up with them from time-to-time to see how they were doing over the next few weeks and months. "It's the human interest story of the century!" he proclaimed.

They realized that this was a gross exaggeration. They both knew that reality didn't work that way. The story would disappear after a short while and that the studio might follow up for a while, but not for long, and that the reports would become increasingly brief and soon disappear. This would be especially true once News Corp received honors for an award-winning story.

The green light on camera number one came on and the interview began. John Doe was questioned first. He said he had recovered his memory of the carjacking, but he had not yet remembered his name. That was why he consented to the broadcast of his earlier interview. He still didn't remember his wife, although she seemed familiar somehow. But he figured that this would return in time. He longed to get back to a normal life. He credited Jeremy Lincoln of Community Mental Health for helping him recover his memories so far, and expressed his gratitude and debt to him for assisting him in being reunited with his wife.

She, of course, said she was happy to find him alive. She knew it would take some time for his memory to return fully and she was devoted to the task of assisting him in the effort. She admitted to feeling somewhat sad that he did not recognize her, but she realized that she was being irrational. She said that she understood logically that he didn't even recognize his own name let alone remember her… yet.

The interview was ended and they were taken to the limo. The driver overheard her telling John Doe about their life together and reassuring him that, in time, he'd remember everything. He said he hoped so, and obviously sounded uncertain while keeping the mask of hope on his face.

The station had agreed not to send reporters and cameras to their home so they could have some privacy, but they couldn't control other news outlets. They provided a decoy couple to depart in another limo that most of the paparazzi followed, but two cars followed them anyway. The driver took evasive maneuvers that eventually lost their tail.

They arrived at their home and she said, "Here we are."

When they pulled up to the house, the driver came around and opened the door for them as they exited the car. They thanked him. He smiled and said, "It's been a pleasure." He waited for them to walk up the sidewalk, open the door, and enter the house before he pulled away.

In an interview some time later, the driver described the ride home. He told reporters that she told him about their lives together and their children. He seemed interested, but not fully comprehending. He said, "She told him, 'this is our home.' He looked interested, but he did not look as though he recognized the place." The driver wondered if he was worried that it might not really be his home or maybe he was afraid he never would remember it. "I hope everything works out for them. It seems like they have a long, difficult road ahead of them."

The Juxtaposition Paradox Charles R. Stern

CHAPTER THIRTY-THREE
The Secret Past

Three months later, Karl and Grace sat in silence for a long time. Nothing moved. The house was still and the weather outside was calmer than it had been in a year. The sun peeked down through the clouds and the Earth kept spinning forward normally.

Finally, Grace smiled. She said, "That worked out pretty well, wouldn't you say?"

"Yeah. Remember when you thought it all up?"

They drifted back into the scene from months before.

****

Grace had tried to speak after a long silence. Her voice was raspy partly from the length of that silence when she hadn't been using her vocal cords and the rest was due to her anxiety that dried her throat. "You know..." She cleared her throat. "Now that I think of it," she said, "when I had to identify your body, you were essentially unrecognizable. Your body was smashed and the car had caught fire. You were so badly burned that I had to identify you by your wedding ring, your wallet, and the fact that you had been in our car when you died. Besides, you had been missing and there was no trace of you anywhere else. And, since I identified you and there was no crime you committed, they didn't do a DNA test on you. What was left of your body was cremated."

"Okay? Sooo." Karl asked. He was puzzled. "What are you getting at?"

"Well, what if…" She thought for a second or two to organize her thoughts. "What if you were carjacked?"

"I see," he said, "but you already identified my body."

"Yeah, so maybe the carjacker stole the car and your wallet and wedding ring."

"Okay, but where was I for all those months?"

"Yeah… that is a fly in the ointment."

They were silent for another seemingly interminable rotation of the Earth. Karl spoke up, "how about this… what if I wandered around with amnesia and lived on the streets as a homeless person?"

"That might work, but why would you have amnesia?"

"The carjacker could have hit me on the head when he took the car, my ring, and my wallet. I already had a blow to my head tonight. I think it was just hard enough to leave a mark that would heal, but there would be a visible scar. It did make me dizzy, too."

"That's plausible. But wouldn't there have been people who saw you or could remember you out on the streets?"

"Yeah, that's a sticking point." Worry and confusion chased the silence around the room again for a few minutes until it crept stealthily back in, collected itself, and pounced like a cat before it was noticed. Karl's brain took the hit. "Hey! I have it!" Karl yelled, before he heard himself.

"What? Spill!" She leaned forward as the lights came up and flooded the room with anticipation.

"Well, I was hit on the head and I had no I.D. right?"

"Right. I get it."

"So, I didn't know who I was and I walked and hitched into the city. I begged for money and food. I slept under overpasses and in churches and school basements, etc. Very few people would have seen me. I hid out, not knowing if I was being pursued. I thought someone was trying to find me and kill me. I worried that they thought I was dead and if they found out I was still alive, they'd come for me again. So I had to keep a low profile and disappear in the city among the larger population there."

"Perfect! You'd have been practically untraceable!"

"Yes, but I'd have to do some of those things to build a backstory."

"Yeah... I suppose, but what?" They thought for a long minute. "But," said Grace, "I could come and get you sometimes and drop you off back there so you don't have to rough it all of the time." She thought for a longer minute trying it on for size to see if it all fit. "But how did you come back if you had amnesia?"

"That's easy," Karl said. "I start having dreams of the carjacking and after a while, I start to remember more and more fragments. In fact, I could, even now, seek help for my amnesia and paranoia from the local community mental health agency. In the city, I could remain anonymous."

"That's perfect! Then you can talk about your amnesia and your fragmented dreams and memories. You could stay in a shelter or more than one so you'd be identified as homeless. You could, through your therapy, slowly remember who you are and you... no... the authorities could contact me."

"Or better yet! The news programs could flash my picture and ask for help from the community to identify me. And all you would have to do is wait for someone else to see me on the news and contact you and/or the police, or even the news reporter!

"The cops and the media would suspect you and me of something funny, but you could say just what you said about identifying me. That I was too mutilated, but the car, the ring, and the wallet cinched it for you. Plus the fact that I never came home or contacted you."

Grace was silent searching her mind for holes in the story. Then she tripped over a bump in the road. "What if they check to see if the DNA is yours? I never did pick up your ashes."

"I think I saw on one of those true crime shows that the DNA is destroyed in the cremation and I was burned in the crash and then cremated. A double whammy!"

"But what if they can get the DNA?" The wind died down, they hit the doldrums, and their sails drooped again. Dreams and fantasies flashed like lightning through the room silently jumping from brain to cloudy brain. The charge electrified Grace and she leaped up and her arms flung themselves as wide as her eyes. "We can just say we have no idea! You know, we can say, what are the odds? Something like that."

"I suppose, but that's kind of flimsy."

Her shoulders shrugged involuntarily, but only for a second before Thor struck her with another bolt. "Sure, but what can they say? You're still here and there's a backstory."

He quickly took up the baton. "I mean, we don't even know why this, whatever this thing is, has been happening in the first place."

"That's for sure."

"Well, I guess that's the best we can come up with," he admitted.

She thought for a moment. "Oh, crap!"

"What?"

"What about the kids? If we're only in this world, the kids would be without us in that world."

"Oh! Right! "Well, I could die in that world too. They would get our life insurances and our investments, as well as the house. They're old enough to be on their own. Joy is ready to graduate from college and she's engaged. She'll soon have her own family. Jimmy has one year left before graduation. We can continue to support the two in this world, too."

"We'll have to pay the insurance company back for the funeral home that conducted the cremation."

"Yeah," he said, "but that seems, under the circumstances, to be worth it. Besides, I can bring some of the money from your death there and use it to pay it back here. No loss!"

"I suppose, but I think of your Joy and Jimmy in the other world having to grieve over two parents especially losing us so close together."

"Yeah, that could be a problem," Karl said. "Maybe I could do the homeless thing here for the backstory for a long time and return to the other house and work there for the income. I'd have to use up all of my sick time, but I think I might be able to manage it for a couple years coming back and forth for the therapy and the rest of the back story. I'd only have to go there at night and take off a couple hours a week to see a therapist." They fell silent for a moment.

"Or, I could just go there during holidays for now. The kids aren't coming home much now anyway. I'd be there when the kids come home from college to visit. I could tell them I'm on business trips at times when I'm here. I could eventually die or disappear there. Of course, it would have to be a situation where I couldn't be found. Maybe lost at sea or something. I could be found alive here like we planned. We could wait until the kids there are settled in their post-college lives. It would just take a couple more years and we can always be together at night."

"Yeah," she said, "as long as we can go back and forth. I don't know how long that will work."

"It'll be difficult to manage, but, if we're careful for a few years, it might work."

"That's assuming," she reiterated, "we can travel back and forth and the door doesn't close."

****

Karl and Grace rematerialized in the future present. They treaded water in the nostalgic reverie of those days that seemed so long ago.

"Yeah, I remember that I was constantly scared we'd be found out back then. I was especially worried when I picked you up at times in front of the shelter."

"Yeah, the bus driver saw you pick me up a couple of times. I had to concoct a story. Fortunately, the social worker was in the process of getting me permanent housing. I told the driver, his name is George, that a worker had picked me up to look and places for me to live. I think he was still suspicious, though. The therapist also got suspicious when he found out I wasn't at the shelter for a few days. I was here with you, but I told him that I was with some homeless woman. I think they bought the stories well enough."

"Yeah, now I get to be anxious because that insurance guy and the cops are trying to investigate us."

The Juxtaposition Paradox Charles R. Stern

CHAPTER THIRTY-FOUR
The Investigation

The police came along with the investigators from the life insurance company to investigate whether a fraud had been perpetrated. They interviewed Karl and Grace separately, but they had rehearsed their story so well that they were identical and completely consistent; their stories were flawless.

Maybe a little too flawless, thought the investigators.

However, they did find some of the people who remembered John Doe when he went by various aliases. They identified his photo. They found George, who verified that he picked John Doe up at the Community Mental Health office and dropped him at the shelter. They easily got written permission from Karl for Jeremy Lincoln to talk about his part in the process of treating him every other week. Some homeless people identified John Doe as being one of their own for a time and confirmed that he slept under an overpass at times and in the shelters. Some of the people who had called in to the news station had left their phone numbers. The ones who had encountered John Doe working for a few days as a dishwasher had admitted that they had indeed worked with him at the restaurants.

The investigators examined the ashes previously assumed to be Karl Otto. They inspected the remains of the burned car, too. The forensics experts didn't find even a small part of bone marrow in one tooth with enough DNA to analyze. They did find an evidence bag with a drop of dried blood from the accident that had apparently spilled onto the street before the car burst into flame where a clairvoyant police officer had collected it. The chain of custody was unbroken for the evidence so there was no doubt of its authenticity. They were able to match it with that of Karl Otto's. They said that their tests and several retests of the DNA taken from the blood was indeed that of Karl Otto. They said that this test is ninety-nine percent accurate. There was a perfect match. This was a complete puzzle. Could Karl Otto have had a twin?

But, the experts said, there would still be some small differences. There was no evidence that he had a twin. Besides, it was unlikely that twins would have the exact same DNA and even more unlikely that a coincidence of a long lost twin would have happened to carjack his brother. The authorities obtained a court order for a forensic examination of Karl, but nothing came of it.

The insurance company could not claim that Grace Otto had lied about her identification even after she said she had to mostly base it on his car, the fact that he was missing, his wallet, and ring because now the DNA was his, too.

Karl had told the media that he had regained most of his memories by the time the investigation was completed and he was to resume work at his company. His bosses had missed the stellar work Karl had done. Because of the massive amount of work Karl had done for the company, they had to hire two people to take his place and they were overloaded. One of them wasn't working out. They immediately accepted Karl back when he called to inquire about his job. So Karl resumed work there with half of the load and they offered a boost in his salary that would result in about three hundred dollars more a week. In some minor way, he was a celebrity, and this, they calculated, would help their business.

In the end, the insurance company demanded their money back. Karl and Grace readily agreed to return it as a way to avoid any further investigations or legal issues. They agreed to repay it over the next three years at a monthly rate with the stipulation that the matter be dropped and no further action would be taken. They put the settlement money from Grace's death into an investment that would accrue a good dividend. So, they actually made money on the deal because of the gains in the investment; and because Karl's raise in pay more than covered the monthly payment to the insurance company.

Karl and Grace had joked about the possibility of fighting the insurance company for the money. They laughed about the difficulty the company would have proving that they had paid for someone else's death when there was overwhelming evidence that it really was Karl who was killed, despite the presence of a live Karl right there in the courtroom who would readily admit that he was indeed Karl Otto. In the end, though, they decided that this would disrupt their lives for years of litigation and public scrutiny. They were afraid that their whole scheme would unravel somehow. So they decided to repay the money so the case could be closed and the whole thing could die a sudden death and be buried and fade into the past with barely a marker on the grave.

Karl and Grace were interviewed on the news about the fact that the DNA of the corpse in the car matched Karl's past and present self and that he had no twin brother. Karl and Grace could only say, "Who knows? Very strange. We don't understand it any more than you do." The insurance investigator and the cops were frustrated, but there was nothing they could do, and closed the case.

For a while after the news of Karl's reappearance and the discovery that he was alive and the DNA evidence proved that he was dead, there were psychics who pontificated and speculated that he was actually dead and that he was really a space alien who took on Karl's exact form. Even that sort of thing died down after a while. Several of the grocery store tabloids contacted Karl and Grace with offers of a lot of money to tell them their story.

Publishers also did this. Ultimately, the tabloids offered more money. Karl and Grace decided that they could tell their concocted story and profit from it. They even hoped the tabloid would exaggerate the story to the extent that no one but the nuts who read it would believe it. At length, this turned out to be true.

They decided to write their own book about their actual experience. They would peddle it to the publishers later. They also decided to write a novel about the real experience but publish it under a *nom de plume*. They laughed about the fake story getting out as the real one and the real one as a magical novel. Grace said, "We have to be careful that we don't make your old therapist feel like a fool."

"Yeah, I'd hate that. He did me some good, though."

"Really? How? You were making it all up!"

"Yeah, but I did the exercises he taught me and it helped me remember the three months gap in my actual memory following your death. I did my own work on it and simply told Jeremy the one we made up. I remembered your death and the cremation, the kids grieving, and the memorial service. He helped me regain almost all of it. So he was a fool, but apparently a wise fool. Of course, I had to explain the tears I couldn't hold back at times, but I made it fit the story I was telling him. Just yesterday I remembered the last pieces of the real story." Karl realized the oxymoron, but the whole thing was an oxymoron! "Living and dead at the same time," he shook his head.

Karl and Grace realized that they would be working harder than ever, but that would bring them closer together while working on their stories. Karl was going to be home more now that he had less work to do at the agency and he could devote more time to writing. The kids were elated that their dad was back. They flew home immediately after Karl and Grace's reunion. They had already headed back to school and wouldn't return until the holidays.

Everything was working out.

"But," Karl said, "We still have to deal with the kids in my old world. What are we going to do?"

There was a long contemplative silence. The lights seemed to dim and the breath in the room slowed and became shallow and dense. Karl and Grace felt their hearts rapidly beating in their chests.

Grace spoke first. "We have to wait for this publicity and any residual legal issues that might emerge to subside."

Karl had felt as though someone was following him. They didn't want to take any chances. Grace had found her way back to his house a couple of times to check on the cat when she was sure no one was following her.

"I think it's safe enough now," said Karl, "for me to go back to my old house and I'll check on the kids. I'll tell them I have to be out of town on business a lot now and that it may be more difficult for them to reach me. I'll tell them that I'll call them every few weeks instead. I'll go there during holidays when they'll come for visits. That way I can keep them in the dark about all of this. The house is paid for; I can pay the taxes from the extra money we have here. I can pay off the car there and pay the utilities too, with this money. I can keep this up until they are settled in their lives and careers. Then I'll disappear."

"How will you do that?" Grace asked.

"I'm not sure, but I'll have at least a couple years to figure it out."

CHAPTER THIRTY-FIVE
Karl Otto Revisited

After the dust settled, the reporters moved on to other so-called 'breaking human interest stories of the century; friends stopped calling about what had happened, and the police and other authorities left him and Grace alone; Karl found his way back to his old house. He went late at night.

He drove around until he heard that music. The weather suddenly shifted and a thunderstorm was brewing. The gap between the lightning and the thunder was narrowing. Rain started to fall. It was nearly five o'clock by the time he made it back to the house. He pushed the button on the remote, the garage door groaned with the burden of reality, but it didn't open. He struggled with key and finally was granted access through the front door. Between the lightning flashes, he noticed that the door seemed to be crumbling. The paint was peeling and the wood appeared to be rotting. *I know I rarely come through this door, but how could it have gotten so bad so fast?*

He flipped the light switch, but there was no illumination save that of the storm. *Did they shut off the electricity? I thought Grace paid the bills when she came here those few times.*

He went to the kitchen and fumbled for a flashlight in the drawer. The drawer handle was loose and nearly fell out. He had to struggle to get the drawer open. It too, was falling apart. He pushed the switch on the flashlight. The light was dim and he had to shake it to get it to come on at all. He noticed the mail on the counter. It was the same as he had left it months ago. He went back to the front door and checked for more, but there was none. *Maybe Grace told the post office to hold it or maybe a neighbor took it in when it started to build up in the box and on the porch.* Grace had visited there on and off when she could evade the press and other gawkers to check on things over the months. After all, they were mainly watching Karl. She would sneak in late at night and leave quickly. But, because of the circumstances, neither of them had been there in more than two weeks. It seemed impossible that there was no mail in all that time.

Karl searched the house with the meager light and saw obvious deterioration throughout the house. Not only was the paint peeling, but there were many signs of structural degradation. The roof had leaked in the bedroom over the bed. There was a huge rusty stain in the middle of the comforter. When he tried to turn on the faucet in the bathroom, the water was struggling to fall out. The ceiling was sagging in the kitchen and in the living room.

"What the...?" Karl muttered. He hoped the kids hadn't been home to see the deterioration of their childhood home.

He wondered about the cat. He was nowhere to be found. The litter boxes were pristine. Grace had left four of them in case they couldn't get back very often. The cat had obviously not been using them and the automatic cat feeder and water dispenser Grace had put in the kitchen that had the capacity to feed the cat for a month appeared to be untouched. *What the hell? Did the cat die or escape?* There was no trace of Algernon.

He dialed his daughter Joy's number. There was a loud screeching sound followed by a message that said there was no such number. *No such number? That's odd. If she had changed her number, it would have at least said that it was changed, disconnected, or that it was a wrong number, but no such number? Besides, she would have told me.* He redialed in the event that it was a misdial, even though he had pushed the preprogrammed number. The result was the same.

He tried calling his son Jimmy, and got the same message. He tried calling their schools to locate them, but he was told that there were no students of those names enrolled and there never had been at either school! He checked their Facebook pages, but there were no Facebook registrations in either of their names. *What the hell? The kids can't be contacted? It's as if they never existed!*

The storm had stopped and the sun was coming up. Its silvery tentacles streamed through the clouds and penetrated the windows. It lit the clouds of dust trailing behind him, stirred by his steps. He looked out at the lawn. It was grown over with weeds. The front steps were crumbling. He heard something crash behind him. He turned and hurried to inspect the situation. The kitchen ceiling had ruptured and fell on the table. He felt the house stagger and creak. *This house is falling apart!*

Fear spread through his body paralyzing him for a moment. He shook it off and ran through the house and out of the front door. He heard more crashing behind him. "Holy sh..." He jumped into his car and started it up, jammed the gears into reverse, and backed down the driveway about fifteen yards and stopped. He watched as the roof caved in and the walls buckled. It wasn't just crumbling, it was being crushed! This caused the windows to burst out with a spectacular explosion of glass. An invisible Godzilla had stomped down on the structure.

He sat there stunned for what seemed like a week, for a few seconds. Everything slowed down to a crawl. It was like a slow motion movie.

He backed out of the driveway and checked the time. It was nearly eight-thirty. The post office would be open soon. He drove there trying to restrain himself from speeding. The postal clerk was just unlocking the door. He asked for his held mail. The clerk disappeared into the back room for what seemed to Karl, about fifteen minutes, but it was probably only five. The clerk returned with a puzzled look distorting his face. "Sir, are you sure you have the correct address?"

"Yes."

"But sir," he said, "there is no mail for that address and I caught the woman who delivers on that street just as she was leaving. She said that she has never delivered mail to that address because it is a vacant lot. She has had flyers that were addressed there by accident, but she never delivered them."

Karl rechecked the address. It was correct. He was speechless for a minute. He reached for his wallet and withdrew his driver's license. He looked at the address; it was faded, but correct. He finally said, "Thanks." And then, as he turned to leave, he said, "I think," under his breath.

He remembered the old lady who was not, he realized, from the cleaning service at work telling him he didn't belong here. *A shadow? Maybe she was right. I never did feel like I fit in here.* He remembered his childhood of 'monkey in the middle', his fascination with the world he thought might be on the other side of the mirror, and the fact that he always felt like an observer in his own life.

He walked quickly to his car, opened the driver's side door. The door alarm went unnoticed. He sat down hard in the seat. He slammed the door shut in frustration with a sense of loss, forgetting to fasten his belt despite the alarm. Karl sat there for a long time just staring.

Finally, he turned the key and the car started. He pulled away from the post office lot. He turned on the radio. *There's that music again!* He turned the corner to where his house used to be. He wanted to see the final destruction or empty lot.

He hit the brakes. There was the house. In fact, it was intact and it did not appear to be worried or in disrepair. He pulled into the driveway, pushed the button on the remote. The garage door opened free of anxiety, the garage light ignited comfortably, and the car drove in quietly and the door closed without incident. Karl sat there in the car with the engine off for a while.

It was then that he sat up straight and wide-eyed, and remembered that both of his kids had been left handed.

Charles R. Stern, Ph.D.

Charles is a psychologist practicing in the Detroit area since 1980. He has also taught at every level of education during his career.

Made in the USA
Charleston, SC
13 December 2015